Tie Died

a quilting cozy

Carol Dean Jones

C&T PUBLISHING
Another Maker Inspired!

Text copyright © 2018 by
Carol Dean Jones

Photography and artwork copyright
© 2018 by C&T Publishing, Inc.

Publisher: Amy Marson

Creative Director: Gailen Runge

Acquisitions Editor: Roxane Cerda

Managing Editor: Liz Aneloski

Project Writer: Teresa Stroin

Technical Editor/Illustrator:
Linda Johnson

Cover/Book Designer: April Mostek

Production Coordinator:
Zinnia Heinzmann

Production Editor: Jennifer Warren

Photo Assistant: Mai Yong Vang

Cover photography by Lucy Glover and
Mai Yong Vang of C&T Publishing, Inc.

Cover quilt: *Tie Died*, 2012,
by the author

Published by C&T Publishing, Inc.,
P.O. Box 1456, Lafayette, CA 94549

Library of Congress Cataloging-in-
Publication Data

Names: Jones, Carol Dean, author.

Title: Tie died : a quilting cozy /
Carol Dean Jones.

Description: Lafayette, CA :
C&T Publishing, Inc., [2018] | Series:
A quilting cozy series ; book 1

Identifiers: LCCN 2018003517 | ISBN
9781617457524 (soft cover)

Subjects: LCSH: Quilting--Fiction. |
Life change events--Fiction. | Murder--
Investigation--Fiction. | GSAFD: Mystery
fiction.

Classification: LCC PS3610.O6224 T54
2018 | DDC 813/.6--dc23

LC record available at https://lccn.loc.
gov/2018003517

POD Edition

A Quilting Cozy Series

by Carol Dean Jones

Dedicated to Phyllis

Acknowledgments

My sincere appreciation goes to my friends Phyllis Inscoe and Janice Packard, as well as to my sister Pamela Kimmell, for all their encouragement, critiques, and suggestions along the way.

Chapter 1

Sarah Miller sat at the window of her new home, watching her unfamiliar neighbors doing the familiar things that people do. She was surrounded by unpacked boxes and furniture scattered here and there with little thought to placement. Her bed was made; Martha, her forty-year-old daughter, had insisted on that. Her medications were on the table. There was food in the refrigerator, and a place setting for one was neatly arranged on the kitchen counter. Again, Martha.

It definitely wasn't Sarah's idea to move from the place that had been home for the past forty-two years. "We worry, Mama," Martha had said in a voice that denoted both concern and annoyance.

Sarah had finally stopped resisting. Martha strongly felt the house was too much for her mother. Perhaps it was. Sarah and Jonathan had moved into the house in the early 70s right after they were married. They'd both been saving for the down payment, and when the little Cape Cod in King's Valley went on the market, Jon was there with an offer. It was a settled neighborhood of small homes built after the war, and it had become a haven for newlyweds and struggling young families.

And a struggling young family was exactly what the Millers had become. Martha was born ten months to the day after their wedding. Sarah left her job at Keller's Market where she had been working since she graduated from high school. Her days at home felt empty at first, but she made friends in the neighborhood, began gardening, and ultimately had little Martha to keep her busy.

Jon never complained about the loss of income but was only making a little over $8,000 a year at the time, which barely covered their mounting expenses. Several years after their son Jason was born, things began to look up. Jon moved up to production manager at the factory, and over the next years, the Millers were able to catch up on their bills and even update their home with a small garage and some landscaping.

Aside from the children, Sarah's greatest joy came from her garden. Having been deeply influenced by reading *The Secret Garden* as a child, she was eager to re-create this dream escape. Over the years, she had planted in such a way that, from early spring until late fall, there were blossoms to enjoy both in the garden and in vases around the house. Jon enclosed her garden with a white picket fence, which she immediately covered with rapidly climbing wild roses. She spent every available hour in her garden, lavishing her plant family with loving care.

Jon had added a garden swing nestled beneath an arbor and intertwined with wisteria. It was there Sarah spent the warm summer days with her family and dreamed of their future. She envisioned the children getting married in her secret garden and the grandchildren who hadn't come yet playing among the flowers. She hoped her grandchildren would learn the magic of nature in this special place. Her garden had become her solace when the children had left home—first her younger child, Jason, and later Martha, who was reluctant to leave the nest.

Dreams. Just dreams, she thought.

* * * * *

Sarah continued to sit at the front window and daydream while watching the goings-on of her neighbors. Each had a small one-story house like hers, with a front door, two windows, and a small porch. All were attached in groups of five. Each had a small square of grass and a tree. Each had a story.

There were several people outside—mostly women, probably in their late sixties—but her attention fell on the couple sitting on the porch across the street. They were older than most of their neighbors. The wife was sewing something, perhaps a quilt. The husband was reading. They rarely spoke, but when they did, their expressions were gentle. Loving, even. Comfortable. There was a calmness about them that came from years of familiarity and a shared life.

I thought Jon and I would be like that couple.

Chapter 2

Sarah spent the next few weeks getting settled. But as she chose new places for her pictures and mementos, she found herself reliving earlier times. School pictures of the children brought a reluctant smile. She wasn't happy about this move, but remembering Martha's soft giggle and Jason's boisterous childhood games softened the pain. Seeing little Arthur's picture caused her heart to ache for her only grandson. He had been gone now for seven years—a second and nearly unbearable loss.

Jon would have loved Arthur. He was so much like Jason as a child.

Thinking about Arthur and Jon led her to the carved cedar chest. She began sorting through the neatly packed contents. She had kept many of Jon's personal items in his old service footlocker; it hadn't been opened for years and sat unopened even now. But the cedar chest was different. It was often opened just to enjoy the endearing memories it held: anniversary cards, letters, and pictures too special to share in the family album.

She held his watch to her heart and sat down on the bed. She allowed herself to remember that summer day eighteen years ago when two uniformed policemen approached the house. One was young and appeared reluctant to climb the two steps up to the front porch. The other was older and more confident, but also appeared somewhat reticent.

"Mrs. Miller?"

"Yes, I'm Sarah Miller," she had said with a smile. She was forty-eight then, but her friends said she looked much younger. She wore her soft blond hair loose and to her shoulders the way Jon liked it. She was wearing a ruffled apron and carrying a basket of freshly cut roses. Jon had invited several people from the plant home for dinner. Sarah loved to have company, although she had few opportunities. The dinner table seemed empty now that the children were grown.

The roast was in the oven, and the sweet smell of freshly baked pies wafted through the screen door. "Just let me put these down." She moved away from the door and returned quickly without the basket. "There. Now, what can I do for you gentlemen?"

Sarah opened the wood framed screen door and joined the men on the porch. As she did, she caught the eye of the youngest officer for just a moment as he lowered his head. In that moment she sensed his distress. She felt her own heart stir as if it were moving to a safer place in her chest.

"I'm Officer Parker," the older officer said gently. *Too gently*, she thought. She felt a stirring in her head, a kind of lightness as if her *knowing* was also searching for a safer place. She felt momentarily unsteady. The older officer reached out for her arm, stopping just short of touching.

"I'm so sorry, Mrs. Miller, but there's been an accident at the factory." He paused. Something moved in the depths of her soul. He caught her just as she collapsed.

Later that day, Sarah found herself in her bed. Martha and Jason were sitting on the settee Jon had bought her for their twentieth anniversary. She had told him that was what she wanted, and she never asked how he was able to find it. Surely he had no idea what a settee was. Maybe Martha helped him.

"Did you?" she asked Martha. Her words were slurred and her eyes unfocused.

"Did I what, Mama?" Martha leaned over her barely conscious mother and gently kissed her cheek. "Did I what?" she repeated softly. Doc Collins had just left, and Martha and Jason were alone with their mother.

Sarah couldn't answer. She wasn't sure what she was asking. *Something about the settee?* And, for a moment, she didn't know why she was in her bed or why the children were there. But like an ocean wave washing over her body, she was suddenly submerged into the remembering. She struggled to catch her breath, but the remembering was too strong…. *an accident … didn't make it … dead. Jon is gone.* Sarah began to sob softly before slipping again into medicated sleep.

Months passed without Jon and without joy.

Chapter 3

"A retirement community?" Sarah had retorted indignantly. "And what about my job?" she added with a stiff smile designed to hide her mounting anger.

Jason had warned Martha that their mother would not take this suggestion well. "It makes sense for her to move to a safer place, but, Martha, you know her," he had said. "She's become fiercely independent since Dad died. Besides, she's fixated on that garden of hers, not to mention her job. She'll work there until she falls over in the produce department. There's no way she'll accept moving to an old folks' home."

"It's not an old folks' home, Jason," Martha argued. "It's a retirement community. She'll have her own house in a neighborhood with other people her age. And when she needs more services, they'll be available. This is perfect for her."

"Well, maybe," Jason conceded. "But she'll never go for it." Martha was determined to try despite her brother's protests. "As for your job, Mother, you're sixty-eight years old. You've worked since Dad died, and you deserve to retire and take life easy. Being on your feet all day is taking a toll on you, and you know it. Your back hurts. Your feet hurt.

Just come with me and look at Cunningham Village. You don't have to commit yourself. Just look."

"Commit myself," Sarah mumbled. "I might as well commit myself before you kids do it for me."

"Come on, Mother. That's crazy. We're just trying to help."

Why is it that grown children think it's helping when they treat you like a child? Sarah wondered.

But in the end, she agreed to go see Cunningham Village. It was just across town. As they pulled past the security kiosk, Sarah spoke for the first time. "This is really compact, isn't it, Martha?" She offered this comment with a smile on her face and just a trace of sarcasm in her voice. "I see little connected houses—rows and rows of them. And I noticed an apartment building touting *assistance with living*, whatever that could possibly mean." The sarcastic tone was building.

Suddenly her eyebrows shot up and with incredulous surprise, she said, "Oh look. I see a nursing home, and …" she continued with mock excitement, "… as we were driving in, didn't I see a cemetery across the way? Very handy indeed. I won't even need to call a cab when I die. I can just walk across the street and heave myself into a hole."

"Mother." Martha stopped the car abruptly and turned to look at her mother, ready for a fight. But instead of defiance, she saw despair in her mother's eyes. She wished she had never taken this on. Jason was probably right. They should just leave her alone. Let her stay where she was and do what she wanted. And they could just continue to worry.

With a sigh, Martha started up the car. "Let's just go home, Mother."

But in the end, Sarah had complied. As she continued to unpack, she quietly wondered why she had succumbed to Martha's insistence. In a way, she knew this was probably the right thing to do. That didn't make it any easier, but as she began to get settled into her new place, things didn't look quite so bleak. Sarah was a strong, resilient woman. She knew she would survive this but wished she could sit in her garden under the wisteria and allow all the new pieces to work their way into a new pattern.

Perhaps there's a little space in the yard where I can make a flower bed. And maybe, just maybe, I'll introduce myself to one of the strangers tomorrow. Or maybe the next day.

Chapter 4

"**W**ell, of course you don't like it here yet. You haven't even been to the center, and you don't know about Saturday night movies or the bus that takes us into town for shopping or any of the trouble we manage to get into." Sophie was a short, rotund woman in her early seventies with a contagious laugh that could be heard up and down the block. She could turn anything that happened in the Village into a comedic episode worthy of a prime-time spot on TV. "Just let me show you around, kiddo."

Sophie was her first and only acquaintance, but certainly not for long. Sophie saw to that. By the end of the week and after two parties thrown by Sophie herself, Sarah had met two or three dozen of Sophie's "closest friends," as Sophie called them.

"Mother, I've called and called. Are you ever home? Where are you? Call me."

Answering machines. Sarah made a mental note to return Martha's call tonight and disconnect that annoying machine. But today she was taking the neighborhood shuttle to the center with Sophie and several of her friends who lived on their block. Sarah's neighbor Andy said he might tag along as well.

The group boarded the little bus at the corner of their street, but at each stop others joined in. Sophie had apparently arranged another party—this one on the road. By the time the group arrived at the center, there were fourteen people, mostly women. Sarah had no idea what to expect of the center. She had only been told, "You'll love it." And *love it* she did.

From the outside, the center appeared to be a large institutional building, which immediately turned her off to the whole idea. But once they went inside, she was amazed. The building had apparently served some other purpose in its previous life, perhaps as a warehouse of some sort, but it had been completely gutted and rebuilt. The ceiling above the lobby was two stories high, and the center of the lobby was filled with plants from the tropics that nearly reached the skylights. As she looked up, she could see an upper-level walkway overlooking the lobby. Andy said there were classrooms up there. Several glass-sided elevators carried people between the two levels.

On the first floor were not only the large lobby but also numerous rooms off of it. Many of the rooms had large interior windows revealing the activities that were going on inside. Sarah saw exercise and ballet classes and a pool with five or six people laughing and swimming together. Four wheelchairs were parked by the pool ladder, and she wondered what it must feel like to be restricted to a rolling chair yet be able to break free in the water. She could sense their joy just by watching them cavorting in the pool.

Continuing around the lobby, there were rooms that appeared to be classrooms. Some were empty, but one in particular caught her attention. "What's this room?" she asked.

"That's our computer lab," Andy offered. "We can use the computers anytime they aren't having a class. Do you have a computer?" he asked.

"I never got one, although my kids thought I should. I was working, and when I was home, I just wanted to be in my garden." Sarah realized this was only a half-truth. For some reason, she frequently rebelled against anything her children told her she should do.

"Have you ever used one?" Andy asked, interrupting her thoughts.

"Well, at the store we had one, but it just kept track of our stock and our hours. Things like that. I could use it for those things but never had a chance to learn anything else. I think I might like to give it a try someday."

Sophie joined the conversation at this point and guided Sarah up the hall to the Resource Room. There she picked up a schedule of classes and told Sarah to check out the computer classes. Andy recommended that she start with the basic class. Sarah felt a tinge of exhilaration she hadn't felt for a long time.

They continued through the center, and Sarah was surprised to find a small grocery store and a coffee shop. Their group had dwindled to five, and they decided to stop for coffee. Conversations at the table were light and unrevealing, except, of course, for Sophie, who had no qualms about telling anyone about anything. She kept the group in stitches with her stories, and at noon she announced it was time to move on to the dining room.

Before she moved to Cunningham Village, Sarah had been told the dining room was one of the features, but she had made a decision to always prepare her own meals, feeling that eating in a congregate dining room would only be appropriate for the very old. But here was a beautiful restaurant with white tablecloths and waiters bustling around. They were seated and offered a menu. Sarah had expected a meal to be wheeled in like they did in the hospital.

"How can they offer this luxurious dining room? We aren't paying enough to cover this." Sarah commented.

"You're right. This is actually not the regular dining room. That's in another part of the building, and dinners there are included with our membership. This is a privately run restaurant, and here we pay. But you won't be paying anything today 'cause we're treating you to the meal of your life."

Sophie motioned for the waiter saying, "Okay, kid. We're ready to start."

The rest of the group had arrived, and tables were pulled together this way and that to make one large, although oddly shaped, table. There was a great deal of commotion as people shuffled around trying to find the perfect seat. But, of course, Sophie was already in it.

Sarah didn't get a chance to order. The dinner had been preordered and was served family style. As she fixed her plate, Sarah listened to the many conversations and the excitement in people's voices, and she realized this was exactly what she needed. Again, she felt that tinge of excitement. Something good was wrapping itself around her protectively.

Some months later, Sarah came to realize that not everyone was having this much fun at Cunningham Village. There were people—some even younger than herself—who never came out of their homes. Some in the assisted living units rarely left their rooms. They had moved into their senior years unable to accept the many losses they had experienced and were collapsing in on themselves. She could see it in their bodies as their heads lowered and their shoulders drooped forward.

"Depression," Sarah had said to Sophie one day when she was speculating about the people who rarely came out of their houses. "I know many of these folks are in poor health and have much to regret and grieve, but if you let the bad times rule your life, it can cause you to fade like a dying flower."

"You think too much." Sophie had retorted with a chuckle as she poured coffee and bit into another pastry.

Chapter 5

Sarah had just finished breakfast and was thinking about signing up for a computer class when the phone rang. "Hi, Andy. Funny you would call right now. I was just looking over the computer class schedule and …"

"That's exactly why I'm calling," he interrupted. "They start next week, and I was going over to sign up. Have you decided what you want to do?"

"I don't know a thing about computers. I was just reading that we need to be learning something completely new as we get older to keep those brain cells firing, so I'm going to give it a try. But …"

Andy interrupted again, saying, "My guide and mentor, Norman Vincent Peale, says all you have to do is picture yourself succeeding, and you will. That's what I did, and you should see me on that computer now."

"You know Norman Vincent Peale?" she asked with astonishment.

"Well … not the real person, actually," he said reluctantly, sounding a bit uncomfortable. "Just the books. But they changed my life back in the 50s when I read my first one. He taught me that you can do it if you can imagine it, and that has been my philosophy all these years. 'Positive thinking,' he calls it. Of course, it didn't help me much on the golf course," he chuckled, "but then I might have been much worse without it."

"Okay, I'll take a lesson from Mr. Peale, and I'll imagine myself as a whiz on that computing machine of theirs. I would love to be able to write letters on it."

"Emails," Andy corrected.

"Okay. Emails," Sarah repeated with a sigh.

* * * * *

Sarah entered the room reluctantly. The few people who were already there had their computers turned on and were actually doing something. She felt intimidated before she even sat down. *If you can picture yourself doing it, you can do it.* Unfortunately, she couldn't stop picturing herself completely destroying the computer with her first touch.

But she didn't destroy it, and, in fact, she learned enough that day to *browse the internet* (new words in her vocabulary) and look up the current weather in her own city and in Tulsa, Oklahoma (for no particular reason other than for the fun of it). She also read parts of the local paper online. By the time class was over, she wanted to know more.

Sarah found all this very exciting. It had always been her nature to enjoy life. But after Jon died, she became despondent for months. She refused invitations and spent many hours in her garden, sometimes just sitting and thinking, sometimes crying, and sometimes working with harried speed as if attempting to meet some unrelenting deadline.

But one day she woke up and heard the birds in her garden, and she realized that life was still good. A few weeks later, Arthur was born. Joyce and Jason were overjoyed to have a son, and Sarah was now a grandmother. She would always have Jon in her heart, but he wouldn't want her to grieve forever. And her new grandson deserved a happy grandma. So she put a smile on her face and dove back into life.

The first thing Sarah did was go to Keller's Market and see if she could get her old job back. Well, it wasn't exactly her old job. Twenty-three years had passed, and the store was filled with all-new faces. But she was only forty-eight and had "energy to burn," people said. So she put on her best outfit, held her head high, and applied for the vacant manager position.

And she got it. It helped that one person was still there: Jacob Myers. Jacob had been a manager when she worked there many years before. He was now at Corporate, and she listed him as a reference. He gave her a glowing one, of course, and called her personally to offer her the job.

Chapter 6

"**Y**ou were on the *internet*?" Martha asked with surprise. "Where? And how?"

Sarah told her daughter about the classes, and of course Martha found a thing or two that could go wrong. "You have to be very careful, Mama."

"I'm enjoying it, and I'm meeting nice people. This is a good thing in my life, Martha." She wanted to add "Please leave it alone" but didn't. *I must remember to buy Martha a copy of Mr. Peale's book.*

"Okay, Mother. Do what you want. But just be careful," she repeated.

Sarah made a weak excuse to end the conversation and curled up in the recliner by the front window, contemplating Martha's warnings and wondering just when it was that Martha became so negative and suspicious. As a child, she had been full of joy. Once Jason was able to run and play, he and Martha had become fast friends and managed to get into more than their share of scraps. But as she got older, she seemed to enjoy life less. She worked as a researcher for the government and put in endless hours on projects Sarah couldn't begin to understand. And Martha told her less and less about her work as time went on.

Martha was married briefly to a man she met in college, but they separated after a couple of years. Martha wouldn't talk about what went wrong, but Sarah always hoped she had someone to talk to about it. It worried her that Martha kept so much inside.

* * * * *

"Okay, I'm here," Andy said strolling into the computer lab. Andy was a slight man, weighing only 145 pounds or so. His steel-gray hair was always in disarray, and he wore faded jeans and a white-and-gray baseball shirt. He probably owned more than just this outfit, but Sophie claimed she'd never seen him in anything else. He pulled a chair over and gave Sarah a quick lesson on sending emails. While he was at it, he took her into several chat rooms. She was instantly intrigued.

"These are all total strangers just talking to each other?" Sarah asked. "I can't understand what they're saying. Is this some sort of code?"

Andy laughed. "Yes, it's the code of young people. I have no idea what they're saying, either. But if you go into a more grown-up chat room, it gets somewhat better. You do need to learn a certain amount of shorthand, but it will come to you. Just watch at first. And be careful," he added. "Don't give out any personal information. You don't really know who you're talking to, no matter what they say."

Since it was the second time she had been told to be careful, she decided she would heed the advice. Sarah spent an increasing amount of time at the lab in addition to her class. She met a few people in chat rooms who wanted to talk to her by email, but she politely refused.

Chapter 7

It was one of those chilly, gray days with steady rain. There were many days like that when she and Jon visited Seattle. He had considered a job there where he would have made more money, but they decided they just couldn't leave their home. Sarah sat in her recliner by the window, a spot that was becoming her place for reflection. Her mind drifted back to Jon's funeral. It, too, was a gray and rainy day.

Distracting herself from the onslaught of pain, Sarah thought about rain and funerals. So often, even in movies, people huddled together, a sea of black umbrellas, as they watched their loved one descend into the soggy earth. So it was for Jon.

During the months following his death, Sarah had tried at various times to pack up his belongings. She was finally able to donate his clothes but had kept his ties and a few of his shirts, hoping to someday learn how to put them into a quilt for Martha. But most of the other things, things she thought of as his treasures, she had simply put in his service footlocker and stored away.

Sarah was reluctant to go through the footlocker. It had not been opened for nearly twenty years, but she felt compelled to take a look today. She gasped when the imagined smell of Jon drifted from inside as she opened the creaking lid. She had forgotten that his uniform and his favorite work shirts were inside. He often said he was unable to make repairs unless he wore one of his tattered shirts. "They bring me luck," he had said with a smile, "and sometimes they even bring me skill."

And sure enough, Jon was always able to find the problem, whether it was a busted pipe or a rattle in the dashboard of his treasured '65 Mustang. As Sarah quietly sobbed, she reluctantly continued to explore through the forgotten items. *Why did I keep this?* She wondered about the many insignificant things she discovered. But in the end she closed the trunk with all its items intact.

Over the next months, Sarah spent much of her time at the center, enjoying her newly discovered obsession: the internet. She and her new cyber friends spoke often, particularly through the garden chat room. One day when she and her new cyber friend, Prissy221, were discussing their past gardens, Prissy said that she lived in a high-rise condo and had her garden in large pots on the balcony.

That reminded Sarah that she had toyed with the idea of a small garden just beyond the concrete patio outside her back door. She discussed the idea with Andy, and he agreed to loosen the soil for her. Together they placed a brick border around the little square of soil to make it more attractive. She then drove to the local nursery and chose a few of her favorite annuals. Andy had offered to drive her there and help her with the planting, but she wanted to do that part alone.

Martha had been adamant about her mother giving up her car. She pointed out that there was adequate transportation in the community, and whenever Sarah needed to go other places, Martha or Jason would be happy to drive her. The car should be sold, Martha had insisted.

Sarah's daughter came by her stubbornness naturally. When Sarah made up her mind, that was it. The car stayed, and Sarah let Martha know that there would be no more discussion about it. Sarah had a strong independent streak that should not be challenged.

When she finished planting her new garden, Sarah settled into the well-worn garden chair she had brought from her home and sipped lemonade while scrutinizing her handiwork. With all her experience, she was able to project herself into the future and see how her garden would develop. She would have to admit, however, that at this moment it appeared a bit scrawny.

Chapter 8

Detective Charles Parker retired in 2008 after more than twenty-five years on the force. Back in 1989, he had been disappointed when the captain had decided to close the Miller case. A brief investigation determined there was no evidence of foul play. The case was closed, and the officers were reassigned. Parker had been uncomfortable with the findings and had tried to persuade the lieutenant to keep the case open, but to no avail. He didn't have much clout in those days, and he didn't make detective for several more years. But he still had a bad feeling about the circumstances. Perhaps he was just hoping to see the lovely Sarah Miller one more time.

Before moving to Colorado, Charles Parker's sister-in-law lived in the Millers's neighborhood, and he often drove by the house, wondering about the pretty widow. Her image would return to his mind: her long flowing hair, her smiling eyes, the basket of flowers. And then her slender frame collapsing in his arms. He hated being the carrier of the news that caused this beautiful woman unbearable pain.

Early in 2006, Parker read about the tragic death of her grandson, Arthur. He contacted Sarah to express his condolences. Much to his surprise, she had remembered him and thanked him for his concern.

The accident had happened just blocks from the boy's home as he biked to a friend's house. He was hit by a speeding car that was never identified. The medics said he had died immediately upon impact; it was little comfort to the family at the time, but in the years to come it was their only solace.

Parker stayed in touch with the investigating officers, hoping something would come up. It never did. He attended the boy's funeral on a cold, rainy day in November, but he sat in the back, out of sight. He didn't want to be a reminder of Sarah's previous loss. He knew only too well the pain of losing a loved one. His Betty had been gone now for many years, and a day never went by that he didn't miss her.

Three years after Detective Parker retired, he suffered a debilitating stroke that left him temporarily unable to speak or move his left side. He was hospitalized for two months and ultimately moved to a nursing home for rehabilitation.

Chapter 9

Despite the fun she was having in her computer class, Sarah was beginning to feel she needed more in her life. She had often passed by the nursing home and wondered about the people she could see sitting in their wheelchairs at the large windows on the second and third floors. She thought that the windows must offer a spectacular view of the community and the mountains in the distance. But heads were lowered as if their laps offered more interest than the view.

One morning Sarah decided this was the day to learn more about the nursing home. As she approached the rather ominous building, she felt a cold shiver as if death were close by. She dismissed the feeling as being her own apprehension, but once inside the facility, she realized death was, in fact, hovering everywhere.

A woman sat in the hall holding a tattered doll to her breast. As Sarah passed her, she realized the woman was softly singing one line of a lullaby over and over. Sarah turned to speak to her but realized the woman was unaware of her presence. She continued to the administrator's office, where she had an appointment to discuss volunteer opportunities. She imagined herself visiting, perhaps playing cards, sitting in the gardens, or just enjoying a few hours with a lonely senior citizen.

By the time she reached the administrator's office, however, she was beginning to realize her imagined visits were far from the reality of life in Cunningham Nursing Home. Mrs. Barnett's tour of the third floor confirmed this. The halls were lined with wheelchairs with gentle restraints holding the shells of their imprisoned passengers. Unseeing eyes stared into nothingness. Occasional cries pierced through the thick smell of hopelessness. None of the residents seemed aware of Sarah passing through their world. *What can I possibly do here?* she wondered.

Back in the safety of Mrs. Barnett's office, Sarah asked about her duties as a volunteer. By this time, she had also seen the second floor and was encouraged to see that there were, indeed, woman and men who still appeared to occupy their bodies. Several smiled at her as she passed by. One man stopped her, thinking she was his sister. He seemed happy to see her, anyway. Looking into the private rooms, she saw pictures and flowers and colorful quilts.

Mrs. Barnett explained that about one-third of the residents of Cunningham Home were indigent. Their care was paid for by the state, and many had no families. They were lonely and frightened. A friendly face, even once a month, would bring them much joy. Mrs. Barnett felt that Sarah would be an excellent resident visitor.

Sarah expressed her concerns, but she agreed to give the idea some serious thought. Mrs. Barnett agreed to begin looking for an appropriate assignment for Sarah. Sarah left the home with mixed feelings, not knowing just why she was both reluctant to pursue this and yet drawn to it.

* * * * *

"*You did what?*" Sophie yelled, sputtering coffee across the table and all over Andy's shirt.

"Watch it," Andy cried, jumping out of her line of fire.

"Why on God's green earth would you want to spend time in that depressing place?" Sophie demanded.

Sarah started to explain, but Sophie immediately cut her off. "Haven't I told you to stop thinking so much? Relax. Enjoy your retirement years. We've all earned the right to just be happy." Sophie sighed and shook her head. "I just don't know what gets into some people. They just go looking for trouble," she muttered as she waddled into the kitchen to refill her coffee cup.

Later Andy walked Sarah home and asked if they could sit on the front porch for a few minutes. Sarah was tired and wanted to enjoy the solitude of her peaceful home, but she agreed to sit down for a few minutes. She had the feeling there was something Andy wanted to talk about.

"You've got to understand Sophie," he began, "and that's no small task. Despite the joke telling and that never-ending cackle of hers, Sophie is hiding a lot of pain. Her husband died in that home last year, and it was after years of watching him sink into the oblivion of Alzheimer's. The last few years he didn't know her, couldn't walk, and couldn't speak, and ultimately he just curled up in a fetal position in his bed, staring without seeing. This went on for many months until he finally just stopped breathing. His passing was a blessing for him and for Sophie."

They both sat quietly, Sarah not knowing what to say. Andy continued, "She never acknowledged what she was going through. She never talks about him. But she'll tell you that she hates that facility and all it stands for."

"I guess that's her way of coping," Sarah said sadly. They sat quietly for a while. Andy finally stood and said goodbye. Sarah felt drained. She wondered if she were making a wrong turn by getting involved at the nursing home. She wondered if she should discuss it with Martha but decided she should make the decision herself. Sarah took a long, hot shower and went to bed.

Chapter 10

Several days later, Sarah was looking through the box of ties she had kept. *How can I possibly make a quilt with these?* she asked herself. *I have no idea where to start.* Then she remembered the center's class schedule and wondered if there was any kind of sewing class. She still had the Singer she had bought when the kids were young. She never did much sewing—just Halloween costumes and an occasional simple curtain for the house. She realized her copy of the class schedule was out of date, so she stopped by the Resource Room later that day.

"Hi there, Sarah," Marjory greeted. "What can we do for you today?" Marjory ran the Resource Room and could always be counted on to steer people to just the right activity.

"Well, I want to find a sewing class. Actually, what I want to sew is a quilt ... but I don't know where to begin. Are there any sewing classes that could help me?"

"We do have a beginning sewing class where you learn how to use your machine, read patterns, and make simple clothing. I'm not sure that's what you want, though."

"No, I can do those things. I want to make a quilt with my husband's ties as a special gift for my daughter." Martha had taken her father's death very hard. She was twenty-three when he died, and she had been the light of his eyes. He had followed Martha's progress closely through college and was anticipating her completion of her graduate studies that spring. It had been an unbearable loss for her. Sarah felt that Martha had never really gotten over it. Perhaps the ties would give her some comfort.

"Well, I have an idea. Do you think you would be interested in the Village Quilt Club?"

"I didn't even know there was a quilt club here. That would be perfect if they're willing to take on a novice."

"I know they would. They took on me." Marjory went on to tell Sarah about the club and how she got involved. "I had just had my twins and was desperate to get out of the house for a few hours. Kevin said we could hire a sitter, and I looked around for what I wanted to do. My best friend, Beth, told me about the quilt club right here in the Village. She decided to share with me that she was secretly making baby quilts for my twins, and she said we could work on them together."

"How great," Sarah remarked. "You had both a teacher and someone to go to the quilt club with."

"Yes, and Beth was so patient with me. She came to my house when the twins were sleeping and taught me how to use the rotary cutter and how to make a very simple four-patch quilt. She shared her tools with me for the first few months, but finally we went to Stitches, and I got my own tools and the beginnings of my stash."

"Stitches? Tools? Stash? So much to learn." Sarah moaned.

"Don't worry. You'll catch on fast." Marjory reassured her. "Stitches is our local quilt shop. Actually, its full name is

Running Stitches, but we all just call it Stitches. It's in town, and the shuttle goes in twice a day. There's a stop right in front of the shop, but it is actually less than a mile and most of us just walk. It's great exercise, and you can go through the park."

"Once you start going to the quilt club," Marjory continued, "you'll find other people who want to go fabric shopping, and you can make it a fun day trip. There's a café right across the street that's a great place for lunch. I'd be happy to drive you to the shop and introduce you."

Marjory went on to tell Sarah about Ruth, the shop owner, and her daughter, Katie, who works with her mother most days. She assured Sarah they could help her get the necessary tools together. "In fact," she added, "they might even be offering a beginning class. We'll ask when we go. Are you free this afternoon?"

"I sure am. When do you get off?"

"In ten minutes," Marjory responded. "This is my half-day. If you can wait a few minutes, we'll go right over there. I need some thread, but I don't ever need an excuse to go fabric shopping."

"Sounds perfect," Sarah said excitedly. "And when does the quilt club meet?"

"They meet on the third Thursday of the month in the evening. You can go with me whenever you want. They meet right here in the center."

"That would be great." While Sarah waited for Marjory to get her things together, she began to feel a bit apprehensive. She hadn't threaded her sewing machine for years and wondered how she would be at quilting. But then she remembered that Andy had said the trick was simply to picture yourself succeeding. So she set her worries aside and, with a confident smile, told herself aloud, "I can do this." Besides, Marjory had assured her that quilters were not only very nice people but also patient with beginners.

After a productive afternoon at the quilt shop, Sarah returned home with several Running Stitches tote bags that were filled with all kinds of quilting supplies and some fabric that she couldn't resist. Ruth had a couple of patterns that she recommended for ties and told Sarah about her beginning quilters' class starting in a few days. Sarah signed up for the class and was excited about her new venture.

As she was unlocking her front door, someone asked, "Why the big smile?" Sarah turned to see Andy walking up the street with soggy clothes and wet hair.

"Well, I'm happy about a new venture, but why are you all wet?"

"Just left the pool. We have water aerobics on Tuesdays. I'm the only man in the class, and I call it *water gossiping* because there's far more of that than aerobics going on," Andy said jokingly. Sarah noticed that, although he was joking, his eyes didn't have their usual sparkle.

"Are you okay?" she asked.

"Never better," Andy responded, and changing the subject, asked, "So, what's your new venture?"

Sarah filled him in on the quilt class at Stitches and her plans to make a quilt with Jonathan's ties. Andy seemed very interested and asked several questions about her plans for the quilt. "Honestly, Andy, I don't have any idea how to do this yet, but I'm hoping to learn in this class."

"Well, let me tell you why I'm asking," Andy responded. "My grandmother made a quilt out of my father's ties.

He worked in downtown Washington, D.C. in the Patent Office. He dressed up every day and was very proud of his tie collection. When he died, my mother kept the ties just like you did, but she didn't know what to do with them. My grandmother, dad's mother, was pretty old by then, but she was a great quilter. She won ribbons in the county fair 'most every year. Well, she took the ties and made a beautiful quilt. I want to show it to you. You might like to make something like that."

"Oh, Andy, I'd love to see it. Can you bring it by this week so I can see it before I start my class?"

"Sure," he said, but then he hesitated and added, "Actually, I'm going away for a few days. Would it be okay to drop by with it this evening?" They agreed he would come by around seven.

Later that evening, Andy rang her doorbell. "I can't stay, Sarah. I realized that I need to get my packing done so I can leave very early in the morning." Andy seemed nervous and distracted. He kept looking up the street toward his house.

"Can't you step in for a few minutes? Maybe just for a cup of coffee?" Sarah asked.

"No," he said emphatically. "I've got to go, but please go ahead and enjoy the quilt and I'll come by for it when I get back. See you next week," he added and rushed off.

As much as Sarah wanted to see the quilt and take it with her to the quilt shop, she mainly wanted to look at it with Andy and hear the stories he had to tell about his father. She put the box in the closet until Andy returned.

Little did she know that she might never have the chance to hear Andy's stories.

Chapter 11

Early the next morning as Sarah was leaving the house, she noticed that there was some sort of commotion up the street but didn't have time to see what was going on. It was going to be a very busy day. Unfortunately, at that very moment, her phone began to ring. She ran back into the house to answer it but decided to let it go to the machine. "Good morning, Ms. Miller. This is Vicky Barnett at the nursing home. I think I may have found the perfect person for you to visit. Please call me when you get a chance."

Sarah sighed. She didn't have time for this right now and still wasn't sure if she wanted to get involved at the nursing home at all. She decided she would stop by Vicky's office after her class, and she hurried off to the computer lab.

Sarah had signed up for a class in word processing. She'd been thinking about writing down some of her memories: a few anecdotes from her childhood perhaps and maybe some thoughts about life with their father—nothing fancy, just some reminiscences that she thought the kids might enjoy reading someday. She often tried to talk about her childhood, but the kids really didn't seem interested. *Maybe someday they will be*, she told herself.

Sarah had taken typing in high school. Of course that was on a manual typewriter, so it was much different from typing on a computer keyboard, but she quickly learned. After a couple of hours of instruction, she felt comfortable enough with the program to start recording some of her memories. She decided not to try to put them in any order. She was just going to type her thoughts as they came to her. The instructor left at 2:30, and at 4:30 Sarah realized she was still sitting there typing. "I need to catch Vicky before she leaves her office," she muttered as she quickly gathered up her papers and hurried over to the nursing home.

"Hi, Vicky. I was hoping you would still be here," Sarah said breathlessly as she rushed into the office. She started to take off her jacket but abruptly stopped and turned to Vicky. "Oh. Is this a good time?" she asked.

"It's a perfect time," Vicky responded with a smile. "And I'm so glad you stopped by. I left a message for you this morning. There's something I wanted to talk about with you." Sarah took her jacket the rest of the way off and sat in the upholstered chair across from Vicky's desk. Vicky continued, "I was aware of your discomfort when you were visiting our in-patient facility, but I had an idea. Last year we had a patient who came to us following a massive stroke. He came here for rehab, but when he was discharged he felt uncomfortable about going back to his home. He decided to put the house on the market and move into one of our homes here in the Village."

"Why does he need a visitor?" Sarah asked.

"Well, even though he's made remarkable progress physically, he's sort of isolated himself. He's a widower, and his children don't live in the area. He seems to be very lonely, and I think he could benefit from an occasional visit or even phone calls. What do you think?"

"I don't know," Sarah responded hesitantly. "I hadn't considered visiting a man."

"Well, if you're worried about your safety, I can tell you he's a retired police officer. If you want, you can always meet in the coffee shop."

"Hmm. It's not that, but let me think about this, and I'll call you back." Sarah knew she would need to mull this over for a few days. *What would I find to talk about with a retired policeman?* she wondered.

* * * * *

As Sarah approached the house, she could hear the phone ringing, but before she could get to it, it stopped. She hung up her jacket and hurried to the phone to see who had called and was surprised to see there were eight other messages. She started playing them, and the first four were from Sophie, sounding very distressed and asking her to call immediately. Sarah decided not to play the rest of the messages and called Sophie.

"*It's about time!*" Sophie yelled into the phone. "You don't know what I've been going through."

"What's going on, Sophie?" Sarah asked, attempting to sound pleasant but actually feeling annoyed with Sophie's impatience.

"Have you heard about Andy?" Sophie asked abruptly.

"No, Sophie. What's happened?" Sarah asked, suddenly attentive.

"He's dead." Sophie sobbed.

"*What?*" Sarah cried, holding her chest and sitting down. "What happened?"

"They found his body early this morning. I've been trying to reach you all day. They're saying it was not an accident. It looks like he might have been murdered."

"How can that be possible? Who would do that? And how could it happen here in a secured community? Does he have family?" Sarah realized she was nervously bombarding Sophie with questions she certainly couldn't answer.

"May I come over?" Sophie asked through her tears.

"Of course. I'll put the coffeepot on. I don't want to be alone either." Sarah hung up the phone and stood motionless. A chill slowly crept up her spine.

Chapter 12

It didn't come as any surprise to Sarah that it was raining on the day of Andy's funeral. The sea of black umbrellas encircled the grave site. Sarah knew nothing about his family but learned the previous night at the viewing that he had an ex-wife and three stepchildren. The children were in their thirties and forties and had children of their own.

Andy's sister was there with her husband. All of Andy's friends from the Village came to the viewing and the funeral. There was some scruffy-looking man at the funeral no one seemed to know. He left immediately after the service, and no one saw him at the cemetery.

Later that day, Sarah was finally able to get a few details and learned Andy had been found in his own living room. The Village security officers noticed that Andy's front door was ajar when they drove past around 2:00 in the morning, and all the lights were on. They assumed he had just stepped outside, but when they returned around 3:00, the door was still open. They stopped and went in and immediately saw Andy lying on the floor in the living room. At first they assumed he had fallen and hit his head; however, once the police arrived, it became apparent that he had been beaten as well.

Sarah and Sophie were devastated by the news of their treasured friend. They both loved Andy. "Who would ever want to hurt Andy?"

Not only did they miss Andy, but they also found it troublesome to know that his murder had happened right on their street. Sarah often took long walks through the community in the evening and felt perfectly safe. She hadn't been out at night since Andy's death and had stopped her evening walks. "Maybe I can find someone to walk with me; at least I wouldn't be out there alone," she told herself one evening. It was right at dusk and a beautiful night. She was tempted to walk anyway but decided to succumb to her fears and stay home.

"A dog." she suddenly exclaimed to herself. "I need a dog."

* * * * *

Although all of Andy's friends were being interviewed by the police, so far no one had any useful information. Andy was liked by everyone and never seemed to have a worry in the world. No one could even speculate as to why he would have been murdered.

While they were gathered in the center for the interviews, Sarah noticed Andy's sister standing alone on the sidelines. Her husband stood nearby but was talking with one of the officers. Sarah approached her and said, "Hello. My name is Sarah Miller. Andy lived up the street from me and was a good friend of mine. I wanted to express my sympathies to you. I know it's hard to lose a loved one."

"Thank you," the sister responded. "I'm Brenda Thompson. That's my husband over there with the officer. I don't know why they keep asking us questions. I haven't seen Andy for two or three years, and of course I haven't seen George since the early 90s."

"George? Who's George?"

"Andy never told you about George?" Brenda asked. "George is his twin brother. They were identical twins but were like night and day."

"Is George here?" Sarah asked, looking around. She was surprised to learn Andy had a brother that he had never mentioned.

"Oh no. George has been in prison for years. He was a difficult child, a wild teenager, and a mean man. Andy and I both kept our distance once we were grown." Brenda hesitated as if trying to decide whether to go on. She then added, "He got into a bar fight in the early 90s and was charged with murder. He negotiated his way down to manslaughter and was sent to prison. I guess he's still there. I don't know and don't want to know." Brenda looked angry.

"Do you think he could have anything to do with Andy's death?" Sarah asked.

Brenda looked surprised but then said, "Well, I assume he's still in prison. I told the detective about him, but he didn't seem particularly interested. I didn't even see him write it down." Sarah thought that was strange but was sure the police would follow up on it.

"Well, Brenda, I just wanted you to know I'm very sorry for your loss. I guess you'll be getting the house ready to sell. If you need any assistance with that, I'd be more than happy to help you. Just give me a call." She handed Brenda a scrap of paper with her name and phone number.

"Thank you, Sarah. I appreciate it. I don't think I'll be doing anything for a few months. My husband has a temporary assignment in Dubai, and I'm going with him." Sarah wondered what her husband did but decided not to ask.

Detective Shields walked up and introduced himself. He asked Sarah to come over to the table where he was conducting interviews. Sarah had already been interviewed by two police officers because it seemed she was the only person Andy told he would be away for a couple of days. She was sorry she hadn't pressed him about where he was going, but she was not one to intrude on another's privacy. He hadn't offered any explanation, and she hadn't pried.

Detective Shields asked her to go over everything she knew about Andy's last day. "Are you sure he didn't say anything about his plans, Mrs. Miller?" the detective asked for the second time. "He simply said he would be away for a few days—nothing about where he was going or why?" Sarah was aware of an accusatory tone in the officer's voice.

"Yes, I'm sure he didn't say any more than that," Sarah responded impatiently. "I've told this to you several times and to the other officers who talked to me. I'm beginning to feel like a suspect."

"Oh? And why is that, Mrs. Miller?" the detective asked, raising one eyebrow.

Exasperated, Sarah said she just wanted to go home, and the detective told her she was free to leave, but she should contact him if she thought of anything else. He gave her his card: Det. Mark Shields. Then, with what sounded like an afterthought, he said, "Don't leave town." Sarah turned to face him looking indignant and was ready to blast him with how she felt about his attitude, but she thought better of it, turned on her heel, and left.

Walking home from the center, Sarah thought about Andy having a twin brother and wondered why he had never mentioned him. Maybe he was just embarrassed about having a brother in prison. She had so many questions for Andy that she would never be able to ask. The loss suddenly washed over her like a wave, and she felt tears welling up in her eyes.

Sarah knew she should allow herself to feel her feelings, but she didn't want to walk down the street sobbing. She was too proud a woman for that, so she attempted to think about something else, at least until she got home. She remembered that she had promised Vicky Barnett she would call about the volunteer job, and she still hadn't decided what to do about it. As she walked, she weighed the pros and cons and suddenly realized something. In the wake of Andy's death and the investigation, it just might be nice to have a retired policeman to talk with about it. She decided to accept the challenge and found herself smiling.

She called Vicky Barnett as soon as she got home and told her she was interested in meeting the client. "I would like to wait a few weeks to meet him, though," she added, "since I'm beginning a quilting class and I'm not sure about my schedule." Vicky was very pleased that she had decided to volunteer. Sarah was relieved to have finally made a decision.

* * * * *

Over the next few days, the investigation seemed to die down somewhat, and people returned to their usual activities. Everyone missed Andy, but as Sophie said, throwing her chubby arms in the air in her exuberant way, "Life goes on."

Not everyone was that nonchalant about Andy's death, and, in fact, it wasn't that insignificant to Sophie either. Over coffee that week, Sophie and Sarah began to speculate on who could possibly have done it. As Sophie talked, tears flooded her eyes. She of course made a joke of it, saying, "Well, there goes the ghost of Andy, squirting water in my eyes."

Sophie and Sarah went through the list of everyone they could think of in the community and found it incredulous that it could be any of their friends or neighbors. For one thing, there was just no motive. They decided it would be good for all his friends to get together at the center and brainstorm. Surely someone knew something that could help them figure this out. Apparently, the police were getting nowhere. They had removed several boxes from Andy's house, including his computer. Sarah briefly wondered why he used the computer lab when he had a computer of his own. He had never mentioned having it.

Sophie managed to get the word out, and the next day the group met at the restaurant. They went first to the coffee shop, but it was immediately apparent that there was much more interest in this discussion than they had anticipated. Word had spread through the community, and twenty-three people showed up—almost everyone on their block and another group of friends he had made in his various activities.

"Truth be known," Sophie was saying, "we really don't know much about Andy and his background. It was news to me that he had an ex-wife and stepchildren." She went on to introduce herself and Sarah and explained that they lived on the same block with Andy. Everyone from that block chimed in with their names, and then they heard from the others.

"Hi, I'm Sam Horner. Andy and I played poker every Saturday at the center with a bunch of the guys from the Village. I probably know more about Andy than anyone because I knew him before I moved here. In fact, he's the reason I chose the Village. We worked together in Pennsylvania at the steel mill in Bethlehem. Andy was a supervisor, and everyone liked him. I never worked for him myself, but we became good friends over the years.

"We would go out after work for a beer," Sam continued. "Andy had just lost his first wife and needed a friend. He was drinking a little too much in those days, probably because of the way he lost his wife. She died in the hospital following an automobile accident. He didn't like to talk about it much, but you could tell he had really loved that woman. He and Mary had only been married a few years when she died. We kept in touch, and when I retired, Andy suggested I come here to live. I'll sure miss that guy." Sam dropped his head and struggled to keep his emotions in check.

"I didn't meet Andy until I moved to the Village," another man began, "but he and I spent many hours together at the coffee shop after our meetings. I know AA is supposed to be anonymous, but I'm not ashamed to say I'm there every week, and Andy would not mind me saying he was an inspiration to everyone there. His drinking had almost ruined his life. He lost his second wife and her kids because of it, but in the years I've known him, he hasn't touched a drop. He became a really great guy that we called our friend." Merrell had not introduced himself, but Sarah had met him once at the computer lab.

A voice from the back spoke up, asking, "Didn't Andy have a brother? I think I remember something about a brother."

Sam responded, saying, "Andy told me he had a twin brother. He didn't have any contact with him though. Andy didn't know if he was even still alive. Last he heard, his brother was in prison somewhere, probably for life."

A woman in the back spoke up, "The ex-wife seemed pretty nice, but she told me she's been out of touch with Andy since the divorce, and she wasn't able to shed any light on what could have happened to him."

"Her kids seemed very sullen," someone added. "I couldn't tell if they were grieving or angry."

A man sitting on the sidelines stood up and introduced himself as Ashton. "I tried to talk to the ex-wife myself. She said the police talked to all three of them the day of the funeral. She was definitely upset about that. I guess the detective had been really rude to her. She said this whole thing was none of her concern and she was sorry she had come. I talked to her awhile but got away as soon as I could. I'm not sure why she came either."

"Did anyone talk to his sister?" Sarah asked.

No one responded right away. Finally, Sophie said, "I spoke with the sister briefly. She hadn't been in touch with Andy for a few years. She left right after the police talked with us, but she'll probably be around later since she's the only person available to take care of Andy's belongings."

"No," Sarah spoke up. "That's one thing I know about. I offered to help her with closing down the house, but she said she would be out of the country for several months and couldn't deal with it right now. She said she would empty it out and put it on the market when she returns."

"Who was that ragtag guy in the back at the funeral?" someone asked. No one seemed to know.

Three hours passed as the group continued to talk about Andy, but no one was able to come up with an idea about his death. "Couldn't this have just been a random robbery gone badly?" one person asked.

"Well, I'm sure the police have looked at that possibility. We do have security, and you need a pass to get through the gates, but I suppose something could go wrong."

The group contemplated that and ultimately decided to break up the meeting. Someone suggested that if anyone had any other ideas, they should contact the group.

"How do we do that?" someone asked. "Who's in charge?" No one volunteered, and finally Sophie spoke up and said, "Sarah and I will be available. Just call either one of us." Sarah gasped. Later she asked Sophie what she could possibly do since she was so new to the Village. Sophie said, "Don't worry about it, kiddo. You have me," and burst out with her infectious cackle.

Chapter 13

Sarah pulled herself out of a deep sleep and felt a great sadness, like something terrible had happened, but until she was completely awake, she wasn't sure what it was. *Andy.* Sarah realized she had been dreaming about the day a group of their friends had gone to the pool and had such a wonderful time. But suddenly, in her dream, Andy began to sink. She grabbed for him, but he slipped away. At first, Sarah was glad it was only a dream, but then she remembered that Andy had, in fact, slipped away and out of their lives.

Once she was up and had coffee, Sarah began to feel better. She was particularly glad this was the day of her first quilting class. She was pleased to have a new venture, but again, she was sad she couldn't share it with Andy. Maybe he knew.

The beginning class was going to meet two times a week. Sarah had the supply list and had purchased everything on her first visit to the shop, but she still hadn't unpacked the supplies. She had opened the bag when she got home that day but was overwhelmed by all the strange items. She decided to set the bag aside and wait for the first class. Ruth had promised her that by the time she finished the class she would know what to do with all the tools and accessories she had in her tote bag and would actually be using them.

Sarah arrived at Running Stitches before the other students. Ruth and her daughter, Katie, were already there setting up the classroom. The shop would be open during class time. Ruth and Katie planned to take turns teaching and taking care of customers.

The classroom was partially exposed to the shop but was in a large alcove that gave them privacy. Ruth liked that visitors to the shop could see the students at work. There were three sewing machines for the students to use if they didn't want to bring their own. Ruth and Katie had also set up an ironing station and a cutting station along the far wall. There were two large worktables in the center of the room.

Ruth was perhaps fifty-five. It was hard to estimate because she was very plain in demeanor and dress. Later Sarah learned that Ruth had been raised *plain* in an Amish community in Ohio. She had left her family when she was barely nineteen to attend art school. Ruth was a talented artist who transitioned in later years to being a talented quilter. Her designs and work were impeccable. Occasionally, one would see a hint of sadness cross her face when people talked about family. She had been shunned by her community and was forbidden to have contact with them. She was particularly sorry that her daughter, Katie, would never know her grandparents or her aunts and uncles in Ohio.

Three other students arrived, and they introduced themselves to one another and gathered around the cappuccino machine, enjoying steaming coffee and sweet rolls. Ruth always had coffee, tea, and sweets available in the back room of the shop, not just for the students but also for the customers. Sarah was clearly the oldest student, with the others appearing to be in their mid thirties.

Probably the youngest was Lacey. Lacey had short dark hair and dark eyes and a flawless complexion. She was nicely dressed in black slacks and a tailored white blouse. She had her baby with her, and Sarah hoped this wasn't going to be a distraction. In fact, he only woke up briefly one time and went right back to sleep when Lacey gently rocked his carriage.

Dottie burst into the shop like a whirlwind, apologizing for being late. Ruth tried to tell her she was actually early, but it was hard to get her attention as she nervously flitted from one thing to another. "My youngest just started school," she explained breathlessly. "I've waited for this day for six years. I just didn't have the time to quilt with two kids in grade school and Mary running around the house, but now that she's in school with the boys, it's my time to have some fun." Dottie was wearing jeans and a rumpled tee-shirt, and her curly red hair was struggling to get free from the scrunchie that attempted to control it.

The fourth student, to Sarah's surprise, was a young man. After speaking with Frank briefly, it was clear that he was somewhat limited, but she wasn't sure just what it was. He spoke slowly and thoughtfully but was very clear about why he was there. "I want to make the little quilt in the window," Frank said emphatically.

Talking with Ruth and Katie later, Sarah learned that Frank had lost his mother when he was very young and had lived with his grandparents since then. His grandfather had recently died, and he wanted to do something special for his grandmother. She had admired the table runner in the window of Running Stitches, and Frank decided to buy it for her. He worked at Keller's Market as a stock clerk and made very little money, but he hoped he could buy it on time. When he came into the shop to talk to Ruth about buying the "little quilt," as he called it, she explained that it was not for sale. It was a table runner that her beginning class would be making. Frank asked if he could take the class and make one. She was unsure what to say.

After talking with Frank for a while, she learned he had attended the local workshop for young adults with special needs. There he had learned to run the sewing machines and worked on a workshop contract making place mats and napkins. Although she was concerned about safety issues, particularly around the rotary cutter, Frank volunteered that he had previously worked in the woodworking shop and understood about being careful. Ruth decided to give it a try and signed him up for the beginning quilting class. Everyone had a supply list and had purchased their supplies in advance, but Ruth had told Frank she had some extra supplies he could use until he decided whether he liked quilting.

"Okay, class. Let's find a seat and get to know each other." It became apparent the students already knew each other from their pre-class coffee break, so she introduced herself and Katie and said, "Let's begin." Ruth started out by showing the class some quilts that had not yet been put together so she could introduce the concepts of a quilt: the pieced top, the batting, the back, the quilting, and the binding. "Now don't be overwhelmed, folks. We do these things one at a time, and what you're going to learn in this session is the basics of quilting and how to use the tools. You'll be making this table runner," she said as she held up the sample that had been in the window. "This will give you the opportunity to learn and practice most of the techniques you'll need to make a large quilt, but you'll be working on something small that you can completely finish in this class. Any questions so far?" she asked.

Sarah spoke up to say she was hoping to make a quilt with her husband's ties and asked if she would be able to do that by the end of this class. "Well, Sarah, as I said, by the end of this class you'll have the basic techniques. So, theoretically, you should be able to make your tie quilt. I think you'll have lots of questions, and you might want to take one more class." Ruth went on to suggest that Sarah take a more advanced class to make a throw or even a full-size quilt. She explained that taking on a project working with silk or polyester ties might be a bit overwhelming this early in the game.

"Another possibility," Ruth continued, "is that you might want to join our Friday night quilt group. It's not a class; it's just an informal group of quilters who come in after the shop closes and work on their own projects. They help each other with quilting problems ..."

"... and every other kind of problem," Katie interjected from the next room.

"Okay, yes," Ruth smiled, "... and every other kind of problem. I think you would enjoy the group even if you haven't started your project. Join us whenever you feel like it." Ruth looked around the room and added, "Of course, that goes for everybody. It's a friendly, casual group, and we would love to have more members."

Sarah was somewhat disappointed but recognized that she needed to learn some skills before she could take on her project. She decided she would sign up for the next level and make a throw for her living room.

Next, Ruth passed out some fabric, and the class practiced with their cutting mats and rotary cutters. They learned the importance of precision cutting. They cut three-inch strips and next went to the machines to practice sewing with a quarter-inch seam. Ruth explained that being precise in these two skills would almost guarantee a well-made quilt.

After a short break, the group returned to the table to find a basket overflowing with fabric. Picking up a few of the fabric pieces, Ruth said, "I've filled this basket with a variety of color values: dark, medium, and light. I've also included designs that are large, medium, and small. Let's go through the fat quarters and put them in piles by value and then by size." The group did the exercise while learning the importance of varying both value and design size. One question seemed to be on everyone's mind, and Sarah ultimately asked, "What, exactly, is a fat quarter?" Ruth explained the difference between fat quarters and quarter yards and when one might prefer one over the other.

"Excuse me, Ruth," Katie interrupted, "Mrs. Morrison has a question for you about some fabric she ordered. I'll take over here." Ruth quickly left the classroom and Katie took her place.

Katie passed out the pattern for the table runner they would be making and went over each step with them. "At the beginning of the pattern, you will see the fabric requirements. Before our next class, you need to get these fabrics. You can purchase them here, or if you have other fabric you want to use, that's fine. Just make sure it's good quality 100% cotton."

"I suggest you choose your border fabric first," she continued while pointing to the border on the sample runner. "This will be your focus fabric, so buy something you like that has several colors in it. Then you can choose the other fabrics on your list to coordinate with your focus fabric."

"Ruth and I will be happy to help you with that today or anytime during the week. I like to prewash my fabric, but many other quilters don't. You decide for yourself. At our next class, we will cut our fabric and begin sewing."

Frank had performed as well as everyone in the class, and Ruth was pleased. "I'd like to come in so you can help me pick out fabric you think my grandmother would like," Frank said before leaving. "I'm not sure she would like what I do."

"I'd be happy to do that with you, Frank. In the meantime, I'd like for you to notice what colors she wears and look around at the colors in her house. See if you can figure out what her favorite colors are, okay?"

Frank left in high spirits. The young mothers went home as well, and Sarah spent another hour looking at the incredible colors and patterns. She was especially attracted to the florals and decided that her next quilt would be a garden in full bloom.

Sarah had such a great time in her class. Walking home, she momentarily thought about telling Andy how excited she was about the class. And then the tears came. She had temporarily forgotten about the tragedy in the Village.

Oh, Andy ... what happened to you?

Chapter 14

A s he walked into the precinct, Detective Shields asked, "Did we get the fingerprint report yet?" He had been late every day this week, and from the look on his face, he was in a foul mood.

"Yes, it just came yesterday," his partner, Detective Gabriel responded. "Nothing useful though. There were lots of prints. The problem is none of them are in the system. There are some small prints, either from a child or maybe a petite woman. And there are prints from a number of other unidentified people. Then there are prints all over the place that are probably Andy's."

"What do you mean 'probably'?" Shields snapped impatiently. "Are they his prints or not?"

"Don't know. The guy was cremated."

"So what? We have his prints from the crime scene investigation," Shields responded. Detective Gabriel hesitated before responding. He knew Shields's patience was running thin. He was not going to like the answer.

"Well, that's the problem. They neglected to print the corpse."

"*What?* How could that happen?"

"New guy ... first dead body. Lots of confusion that night. Everyone thought someone else had done it. Believe me, there are *no* fingerprints of the corpse."

"Well, I'll be damned. The lieutenant is going to be on my butt for this one."

"It's not your fault, Mark. Ease up. The prints that are all over the house have to be Andy's. He lived there. They're on the bathtub, the towel rack, the silverware, the freezer door ... everywhere. Besides that, the neighbors and the sister identified the body. It was Andy Burgess."

Detective Shields slid his lower desk drawer open and removed a silver flask. Gabriel watched him fill his coffee cup. He returned the flask to the desk and downed most of the contents in a single swallow. He closed his eyes for a few moments and then turned to Gabriel and said, "We can handle this."

"There's one other thing," Gabriel added, reluctantly.

Shields looked at him as if he were daring him to speak, but then he demanded, "What is it?"

"There are some places that should have prints, but they don't. It's not so much like they've been wiped clean, but more like someone was wearing gloves and the existing prints were smeared. I'm thinking there was someone else in that place—maybe looking for something."

"Well, brilliant," Mark said sarcastically as he drained the coffee cup. "Of course there was someone else there—the killer!"

At the risk of irritating Shields even more, Gabriel went on to say, "Yes, the killer. But I think the killer was looking for something and knew he could be identified."

* * * *

"Hi Sarah, this is Marjory from the Resource Room. I was wondering if you still want to go to the Village Quilt Club meeting. It's tonight." Sarah picked up the message in the midafternoon and was feeling a bit overwhelmed. She wondered if the quilt club, the classes, and volunteering were going to take up too much of her time. She still wanted time to spend with Sophie. She felt there must be some way they could help find out what happened to Andy.

But after some thought, she realized that she could always drop some of the quilting activities if they proved to be too much. The volunteer job was a commitment she would need to make if she was going to do it at all.

Ultimately, she called Vicky at the Volunteer Office to say she would begin her volunteer assignment on the first of the month and asked Vicky to set up a meeting for the first Monday at the coffee shop.

Then she called Marjory and said she would love to go to the quilt club meeting.

That night, after returning home from the quilt club, there was a message on her machine. "I've been debating whether to mention this, but when I saw Andy at the pool last week he really wasn't himself. He seemed worried about something. I tried to talk to him about it, but he just brushed me off saying, 'Oh, I just had a rough night.' This isn't much, but do you think I should report it to the police? It's probably nothing and wouldn't help them at all. What do you think?" The caller left her name and number. Sarah decided not to call her back this late and to discuss it with Sophie the next day.

Sarah was tired and went right to bed but found she couldn't sleep. She began thinking about the quilt club and how advanced all the quilters were. "Will I ever be able to make such beautiful quilts?" she asked herself. It had been show-and-tell night, and everyone brought their latest works of art.

There were more people at the club than Sarah had expected. "I had no idea there were this many quilters in the Village," she whispered to Marjory. Marjory explained that the club was open to the whole community and not restricted just to residents of the Village.

Sarah wished she had her camera with her so she could remember the incredible designs. She took lots of notes but was sure she wouldn't be able to remember it all. She jotted down the names of some of the patterns and some of the color schemes. One woman had made an incredibly striking Log Cabin quilt in purples and greens and had a second one she was working on that she said was an Ohio Star.

Five or six women lined up to show the quilts they had made at their annual quilt retreat. Their quilts were all the same pattern, the Triple Irish Chain, but amazingly they all looked very different. One was made with blue, rose, and brown on a cream background. Another woman explained she had made hers from her *scrap bag*, and it had the look of an heirloom, even though she had made it just last month. Sarah was beginning to see the importance of color and fabric choice when planning a quilt.

They had a speaker who did longarm quilting. She laid out samples of her work and invited members to come by her house and see the machine in action. She passed out her cards, and for the first time Sarah realized there was more to making a quilt than just designing and sewing the top. Unless she wanted to learn how to machine quilt or maybe hand quilt, she was going to need a longarm quilter. She tucked the card into her purse.

During the break, Marjory introduced Sarah to some of the other members and told them Sarah was a new quilter. Sarah was immediately impressed with how willing the women were to help her. She added several other numbers to her purse and excitedly began talking about her dream to make a tie quilt using her deceased husband's ties. Several of the women had made tie quilts in the past and promised to bring them to the next meeting so she could see how they did theirs.

One thing that became very clear at the meeting was that she had lots to learn. She was going to need more classes at Stitches than she had originally anticipated. She was also going to need a lot more ties.

Sarah finally fell asleep and slept soundly until the phone rang the next morning.

Chapter 15

The phone rang while Sarah was still in that twilight state between dreaming and reality, not quite awake and not quite asleep. She stumbled to the phone and saw that it was Sophie. "Sophie. What are you doing up so early? I usually don't see your shades go up before eight. What time is it anyway?"

"Well, if you're asking that, then I guess I woke you up. It's almost six. I just had to call. I couldn't wait any longer. You were out last night when the police came by."

"The police? Why were they here?" Sarah asked. She was still a bit blurry eyed but slipped on her robe and went into the kitchen to start the coffee.

"It was that Detective Shields. He has a way about him that makes you want to confess even if you haven't done a thing."

"What did he want?"

Sophie sighed deeply and said he had come by around seven the night before. She asked him why he was working so late and he said they were interviewing everyone again. He said they're beginning to suspect it was an "inside job," as he so eloquently put it.

"What?" exclaimed Sarah. "An inside job? What does he think this is, a community of hardened criminals disguised as old people? I'm angry with that man all over again."

"Well, he did explain how he came to this conclusion, and I must admit, it makes some sense," Sophie said rather reluctantly.

"Makes some sense? How can that possibly …" Sarah paused. "… wait a minute. Why are we talking about this on the phone at the crack of dawn? Come on over. I'll put the coffee on."

A few minutes later, Sophie burst through the door in her hot-pink elephant pajamas and her green trench coat. She slipped her coat off and dropped it across a chair, revealing the tattered purple nightshirt she had pulled on over her pajamas.

"I hope this isn't what you were wearing when the good detective arrived last night," Sarah jokingly commented.

"Well, this is exactly what I was wearing, and he can just arrest me for unlawful fashion." She poured herself a cup of coffee and helped herself to several of the oatmeal cookies Sarah had placed on the table. "I always eat oatmeal for breakfast," she offered. "It's very good for you, you know."

"Okay, Sophie. Swallow that mouthful and tell me what you were talking about earlier."

"Okay, here's the thing. The police have reviewed all the tapes for the day that Andy was killed."

"What tapes?"

"… from the cameras at the gates," Sophie explained. "The gate has cameras going 24-7. According to Shields, no one entered the Village who didn't belong here. Two people had visitors, and they had permission to come. Otherwise, there were only residents who came and went. They even checked several days before and after his death just to be sure."

"Well, that doesn't mean it was one of us. Isn't there another way to get in?" Sarah asked.

"Actually, no. You can only get into the Village by the gate. But just in case, Detective Shields told me that they also checked every inch of the fence to make sure there were no breaks. We're really very well protected here," Sophie proudly pointed out.

"Not too protected," Sarah observed. "Andy was murdered here."

They drank coffee and quietly thought about this new development. Sophie had a few more cookies. Eventually, Sarah spoke up, saying emphatically, "Well, no one from the Village could have done this. No one from here would do that."

"… and you know everyone from here, I take it?" Sophie asked sarcastically.

"Well, no …"

"So? Maybe it *was* someone from here. Maybe we need to broaden our net and talk to more people. Someone must know something."

"Oh my. I completely forgot something I wanted to tell you," Sarah stated abruptly. "Someone called me last night. Now, where did I put that piece of paper …?" She searched around the cabinet by the kitchen phone where she collected papers and bills awaiting action. "Here it is. This lady called and said she wanted my advice about whether to talk to the police."

"Who was it?" Sophie asked.

"It was a woman named Millie. Millie Lake."

"I know Millie. We've all known Millie and Ralph since we moved here. Did she have some information?" Sophie asked and continued without waiting for an answer. "Maybe we can talk to her before the police. Go call her. We'll go right over."

"Slow down, Sophie. First of all, she just said that she thought Andy looked troubled last week. And second of all, look at you. You aren't dressed to call on anyone. I think I'll call her and tell her she should contact Detective Shields and report what she knows. Then I'll ask her if we can stop by later today and talk to her. Okay?" Sophie nodded while reaching for another cookie.

Later that day, the two women arrived at Millie Lake's house. Millie seemed very shaken and admitted that she hadn't called Detective Shields as Sarah had suggested. She offered the women tea, and both accepted, thinking it might help Millie calm down if she had something to keep her occupied.

Sarah and Sophie sat down at the kitchen table. Sarah brought up the subject while Millie prepared the tea. "Tell me, Millie. Why didn't you call the detective?"

"I was just too nervous," Millie admitted. "I was hoping you would do it for me."

"Well, Millie, I'd be happy to place the call and tell Detective Shields that you have something to tell him, but then you really need to tell your story directly to him."

Sophie spoke up and asked, "Would it help to tell us first?" Sarah shot her a look, knowing that she was dying of curiosity and wanted to hear the story as soon as possible.

"Yes, it would," Millie said, somewhat relieved. She put the steeping teapot on the table along with the cups and began talking. She seemed reluctant to talk about it at first but became more animated as she talked. She explained that she and Andy took water aerobics together. The day before he was killed, he seemed different. Usually he was helping people into the pool and showing newcomers the moves. But that day he just stayed to himself. He didn't work out energetically and seemed very preoccupied. When his cell phone rang, he jumped out of the pool, grabbed the phone, and moved to the far corner of the room. "I wasn't able to hear what he was saying, but he didn't get back in the pool. He just left without a word to anyone. In fact, I didn't even see him dry off. He just pulled his jeans and tee-shirt on and left."

"How long was that before he was murdered?" Sarah asked.

"A day or two, I guess. Maybe the same day. He was found Thursday, wasn't he?" Millie asked.

"Yes. Thursday night very late, as I understand it," Sarah replied. "Sometime before morning. The Village security folks saw the door open and the lights on all night."

"Well, then it must have been our Thursday class—the day he was killed, I guess," Millie said with tears welling up in her eyes.

The three women sipped their tea and talked about the fact that the police needed to know this. "It isn't much," Sarah said, "but they need to know everything. That phone call could be important, and they have ways to find out who he was calling."

Before they left, Sarah placed a call to Detective Shields. Millie spoke to him briefly, but she began to sob. Sarah took the phone and explained that Millie was too upset to talk right then, and she went on to tell him the gist of what Millie had said. As she suspected, Shields said he would need to speak to her in person and agreed to come to her house later in the day. Sarah gave him the address and hung up. Millie pleaded with the two women to stay with her until he came, but Sarah said she had other commitments and had to leave. They both assured her she would do fine. "Just tell him exactly what you told us," Sophie said.

"Why do you think she's so upset?" Sarah asked Sophie after they left. "She was only reporting that Andy seemed distracted. I don't understand the intensity of her reaction."

"I have no idea. She seems scared. I think there's much more to the story than she's telling us. Maybe the good detective can beat it out of her," Sophie suggested. "He can probably even get her to confess to the murder … and maybe several others," she added sarcastically.

Sarah ignored Sophie's sarcasm and said, "Well, she's very high-strung. Just the thought of talking to the police seems to terrify her. But I don't have the time to stay there until he shows up." Besides, something about the woman was bothering her.

After she dropped Sophie off, Sarah went home and pulled out her writing pad. She was beginning to feel overwhelmed and needed to sit down and make a list of what she needed to do. She jotted down the following items: make an appointment with Detective Shields regarding their progress, buy fabrics for the next class, get a dog, solve Andy's murder, and call Martha and Jason about coming to dinner. She looked at her list and wondered if she should throw it away. *If anyone reads this list*, she told herself, *they will certainly think I'm losing my sanity.*

Chapter 16

The next morning she picked up her list, and her eyes went directly to one item. "Get a dog." Sarah hadn't had a dog since she was a child, but once she started thinking about getting one for protection, it caused her to reflect on all the fun she had with Max, her border collie.

Maxine was an energetic dog, and Sarah doubted that she could, at her age, keep up with another one like Max. But she had been Sarah's very best friend all through school. She would rush home to get Max so they could leave on one of their many adventures through the fields and woods surrounding her childhood home. Maxine always looked at Sarah with such love in her eyes. Jon had often looked at her in that same way.

Feeling she had strayed far afield from the tasks at hand, Sarah returned to her list. Nothing really appealed to her on the list except looking for a dog. Setting the list aside, she decided to go to the pound and just walk through. *Not to get a dog today, of course*, she told herself emphatically. *Just to look around.* She thought about inviting Sophie to go with her but decided this was something she should do alone.

Sarah entered the animal shelter hesitantly. The young people at the counter were kidding around and didn't notice her right away. A young man in a red tee-shirt and jeans suddenly looked up. With a bright smile, he said, "Good morning. I'm Bill, and this is Nancy. What can we do for you today?"

Sarah explained she was just there to look and that she was in the early stages of thinking about adopting a dog. The three talked awhile about what she was looking for. Nancy slid off of her stool and stood, revealing that, although she seemed to be the older of the two, she barely reached to Bill's shoulder. They both appeared to be about fifteen, but all young adults looked to be about fifteen to Sarah now that she was approaching seventy. She thought about how old she must look to them with her short gray hair, polyester pants, and sensible shoes.

They entered the kennel, and Sarah immediately felt despair. It was in the air around them. *Hopelessness. This is what I felt in the nursing home*, she realized. For a moment, Sarah reflected on the similarity between the kennel and the nursing home. The outcast and the unwanted. *How great it would be if the two could get together and comfort one another.*

Sarah had no idea what kind of dog she was looking for. When they had asked her earlier, she had said she wanted a dog for protection and companionship. Bill said, "Well, we should be able to find you a dog that can do that. In fact, that's what dogs do best."

The first few dogs she passed by were very large. "I don't think I'm strong enough to handle such a big dog," she said, mostly to herself.

Then they came to an adorable little poodle cavorting around in his cage. He stood on his hind legs and hopped in circles appearing to be saying, "Look at me. Look at me!" But Sarah immediately knew she didn't want to add that level of energy to her quiet home.

Several dogs looked at her with what she felt were pleading eyes. It broke her heart to break eye contact with them and continue walking. She wished she could save them all. As she approached the last row, she hadn't seen a dog that she felt was right for her. But she saw many dogs, and she wondered who their owners had been and how they could have abandoned them.

"What kind of person is able to turn their back on these dear creatures?" she asked.

Nancy spoke up and explained that there were many reasons for people to give up their dogs. "People move away and feel they can't take their dogs. People get sick and can't care for them. Some of these dogs were taken away from their owners because they were abused or neglected. Some were simply born on the street and never had a home. We try our best to find homes for them," she explained. "Also, there are some rescue organizations that take them from us and put them in foster homes until they can be adopted."

"What happens to the ones that don't get adopted?" was on the tip of her tongue, but she decided not to ask. She didn't want to hear the answer, and she didn't want Bill and Nancy to have to say it. They clearly loved every animal in the shelter. Nancy had a treat in her pocket for each and every one of them as they walked through. Bill went inside one cage where the dog hadn't come to the door to greet them, and he stroked the dog gently. "Depression," he said sadly as he exited the cage, "It's common here."

Just like in the nursing home.

Sarah left almost as depressed as the animals. Bill and Nancy encouraged her to come back. They took her name and number in case a dog came in that they thought would be right for her.

On her way home, she decided to stop by Stitches. Playing with fabric would certainly improve her mood. It was fascinating to her that she was so quickly getting caught up in the world of quilting. She loved looking at and touching fabric, especially in Ruth's shop. Ruth had her fabric organized by color so that, when you entered the shop, you were dazzled by a beautiful rainbow of colors that ran from the left side of the shop to the right. She even had a large, gold-toned flowerpot at the far right, and her customers jokingly called it the "pot of gold at the end of her rainbow."

Ruth only carried cotton of the very best quality. And, of course, she carried all the accessories a quilter might need. The accessories hung on a large pegboard just beyond the fabric section: rulers of all shapes and sizes, rotary cutters and blades, needles, pins, and even some items Sarah hadn't learned how to use yet. Beyond that was a large rack that held every possible shade of thread. Marjory had encouraged Sarah to start with black, white, gray, and beige, explaining that these colors would cover most of her needs unless she was doing top stitching or quilting.

Ruth didn't carry sewing machines. She had the large back room where she could display them, but she preferred to keep that room for classes. Ruth loved teaching classes and watching novices become expert quilters before her eyes.

Sarah took out her pattern and read the fabric requirements. She remembered that Katie had said to choose her focus fabric first. After much searching and piling bolts side by side to see the effect, she decided on a fabric with a crocus design in blues and purples with a soft green background. With Ruth's help, she chose coordinating fabrics and thread for the rest of the project.

Ecstatic, Sarah left the shop and headed for the center. First she stopped by the Resource Room to show Marjory her purchases. She then stopped at the Volunteer Office to talk with Vicky about the person she would be visiting. Their visits would be starting in a couple of weeks, and Sarah was beginning to get nervous about it. She wondered if she could find things to talk about.

Vicky had told her he was a retired policeman, and Sarah feared the two of them wouldn't have much to talk about. She had hoped she would be visiting a woman so they could talk about kids and cooking and all the things they might have in common. But then she remembered that perhaps he could give her some ideas about Andy's case.

Sarah's phone was ringing as she was unlocking the front door, but the call had already gone to the machine by the time she got in. *I'll pick it up later*, she told herself as she hung up her jacket.

Chapter 17

Early the next morning, Sarah remembered she hadn't picked up the message from the day before. She made coffee and toast with peanut butter and sat down at the kitchen table to check the machine. In fact, there were two calls she had missed. The first was from Detective Shields, and she remembered that she had intended to stop in and see him yesterday. Now he wanted to see her. She wondered why but made a note to call him after nine. It was still very early.

The second call was from Sophie, who said she had heard from Detective Shields. She was upset by the call and wanted to talk to Sarah about it. Sarah called Sophie and told her to come on over for coffee.

"… and?" Sophie asked.

"What do you mean?" Sarah asked confused.

"Come by for coffee and what?" Sophie responded impatiently.

"Well, I'm having toast and peanut butter. You're welcome to join me."

"Peanut butter," exclaimed Sophie. "I outgrew peanut butter sixty years ago. I'll bring donuts."

After bursting into Sarah's kitchen in her usual loud, chaotic manner, Sophie sat down with several jelly-filled donuts and poured herself a cup of coffee. Sarah freshened up her own coffee and said, "Okay, Sophie. What's going on now?"

"Well," she began, with jelly on her face and another donut in her hand, "our favorite civil servant, Detective Mark Shields, called yesterday and essentially *ordered* us to meet with him downtown today at 10:00 sharp."

"What in the world for?" asked Sarah, looking somewhat irritated.

"He said he has two things to discuss with us, and that's all he would say. He hung up without even a goodbye."

"Are you going?" Sarah asked.

"Of course I'm going. Do you want to be arrested for disobeying a police officer?"

"Sophie, I don't think that's a crime. We aren't suspects. At least, I don't think we are." They finished their coffee and Sarah, feeling somewhat unsettled, told Sophie to go home and get ready, and she would drive them into town. "Let's just get this over with." She decided not to call Shields back and just hear what he wanted to say in person.

* * * * *

"Good morning, ladies," Detective Shields greeted them without a smile as they were escorted into his office on the second floor. "Thank you for coming," he added without looking at them.

"We had a choice?" Sophie asked sardonically. Sarah made a mental note to talk to Sophie about that tone of hers. She was going to get them both into trouble one day.

Detective Shields ignored the comment and began, "I wanted to speak with both of you about two things that concern me."

Sarah shifted in her chair a bit and rearranged her purse on her lap. Sophie stared him in the eye and asked in an icy tone, "Oh? And what would those two things be?"

"I want to talk to you about interviewing suspects on your own and about withholding vital information about this investigation." Detective Shields was frowning but looking down at his desk blotter.

"Interviewing suspects. Withholding information." Sophie demanded, "What are you talking about?"

Sarah was speechless. When she finally pulled herself together enough to speak, she said, "Can you please start with your second accusation? What information have we withheld?"

"Okay, we'll start there. You were quick to tell me that Millie Lake wanted to share some information with me. And it turned out to be some inconsequential information, to say the least. What you didn't tell me was that Millie was having an affair with Andy prior to his death."

Sophie couldn't resist. "Well, of course it was prior to his death. Who has affairs once they're dead?"

Sarah, hoping to take attention off Sophie's sarcasm, spoke up saying, "Affair? I don't believe that. Where did you hear such a thing?"

Shields ignored her question and remained silent, apparently waiting for the two women to respond. Sarah hesitated a moment to get her bearings and added, "Hold on. I knew Andy well. I counted him among my closest friends.

I don't believe he was having an affair—particularly not with a married woman."

Shields turned to Sophie, "And you, Mrs. Ward, you didn't know about this either?" Sarah had never heard Sophie called "Mrs. Ward" and was a bit taken aback. She was also surprised when Sophie did not respond immediately. "Well, Mrs. Ward, did you know?"

"Okay. I didn't actually *know* in the sense that you mean. What I mean is he never told me. Millie never told me. But you know ..." she stumbled a bit with her words. "Maybe I wondered ..."

"And what made you wonder?" he asked in his accusatory tone.

"Well, little stuff, I guess. They talked to each other a lot. They sat together in the coffee shop. That kind of stuff, I suppose. I don't think I would have thought of it on my own, but there was talk, you know—gossip. But that's sure not something to go to the police with." Sophie drew herself up in her chair indignantly. "Anyway, I'm sure it wasn't true."

"Okay, let's set that aside for the time being. Why are you two running around interviewing suspects?"

"Interviewing suspects?" Sophie bellowed, jumping up out of her chair. "When did Millie become a suspect?" she demanded.

Shields ignored the question. "So why were you talking to her?" he asked. Everyone remained silent.

Finally, Sarah spoke up, saying, "Millie called me the other night and told me she wanted to know if she should tell you about Andy getting a phone call the day before he was killed. She said he was upset by it, and she wondered if that was something you should know about. I told her to call you and let you know."

"Later that day, we got worried that she might not call, and we went over to talk with her," Sarah continued. "And sure enough, she hadn't called. That's when I dialed your number and put her on the phone." Sarah hesitated long enough to look at Shields and attempt to determine how he was reacting to what they were saying. As usual, he was a blank slate. She continued, "We stayed while she talked to you just to make sure she followed through." Sarah was now the one to sit very straight and look indignant.

Sophie had sat back down but was clearly outraged. "I don't like the direction this whole conversation is taking," she said, as she again stood. "It's time for us to leave," and she confidently headed for the door.

Trying to smooth things over as they left the office, Sarah turned and smiled, saying, "Would you please let us know if you find out anything?"

This was clearly not the right choice of words. Shields got red in the face and appeared barely able to contain his anger. "I will not be reporting to either of you about the Department's progress, but if I need any additional information, I will certainly contact you."

As they walked down the wall toward the elevator, Sophie whispered, "Did he just tell us to mind our own business?"

"Yes, I believe the whole meeting boils down to that," Sarah responded.

"I'm sorry, dear," Sophie responded, "but Andy's death *is* my business, and I intend to follow wherever the clues lead me. Are you with me?"

"Of course I am."

As they approached the elevator, the doors opened and two officers exited, one on each side of Ralph Lake, Millie's husband. "Good Lord," Sarah exclaimed when they were out of earshot. "I hadn't taken this new evidence to its logical next step."

"Are you thinking Ralph could kill Andy? They've been friends for years."

"Friendships are often lost over money and love," Sarah philosophized. "In fact, *lives* are often lost over money and love."

They were headed home, but they decided to stop at the café across the street from Running Stitches. It was close to lunchtime, and the café was beginning to fill up. They found a booth toward the back and ordered the daily special. For the next hour, the two women put their heads together and tried to make sense of it all.

Chapter 18

Detective Shields sighed deeply as the women left his office. He slid his bottom drawer open and pulled out the flask. He toyed with it, thinking about the promise he had made himself yesterday. And the day before. And the day before that. He shouldn't be drinking on the job, but it seemed like every little problem attached itself to his desire. He looked around at the empty office as if he were expecting to see someone. No one was there, of course. He opened the flask and quickly topped off his half-full coffee cup. The leftover coffee was cold, but the whiskey warmed his throat and eased his craving.

He thought about the case. The body was bruised as if the victim had been severely beaten, and the hands were bruised as if he had been attempting to defend himself. Petite, demure Millie Lake couldn't have done it. But the husband? Did he find out about the affair? And since it looked like an inside job, inside Cunningham Village, he appeared to be the most likely suspect.

About that time, Detective Gabriel tapped on the door and walked in with a burly and apparently very angry man. A second officer did not enter but stood near the door.

The door was left open. Detective Gabriel introduced the man as Ralph Lake and asked him to sit down. When Lake started to argue, Gabriel suggested they move to a formal interview room.

"I'd like to talk to Mr. Lake here in my office if he'll cooperate. Otherwise, we can move to an interrogation room," Detective Shields said to his partner. "We're just looking for some information," he added, directing this comment to Lake. "Let's keep it informal. Please sit down, Mr. Lake. You, too, Detective Gabriel."

They both sat, Gabriel to Shield's left and Lake on a chair farthest from Shield's desk and against the wall. Ralph Lake looked the detective directly in the eye. Neither flinched. Finally, Ralph looked down momentarily, adjusted his pant leg, and said, "Okay, so why am I here?"

"You are here because your name came up during the investigation of Andy Burgess's death. What can you tell us about your relationship with Mr. Burgess?"

"Relationship." Lake spat the word as if it left a bad taste behind. "Relationship," he repeated in a quieter tone as he lowered his head. With his head still down, he continued, "I had no relationship with that guy. I hardly knew him. Well ... at one time I thought I knew him ... but I didn't."

A long period of silence followed. "And when did you discover you didn't know him the way you thought you did?" More silence.

Finally, Ralph Lake spoke slowly, choosing his words carefully. "I met Andy maybe ten years ago. Him and me, we used to work in the lumberyard outside of town. We helped build that dang place where we live now, Cunningham Village." More silence.

After a while, Shields said, "Go ahead."

"Well, at first we hung out together. He was drinking a lot. So was I, for that matter." Detective Shields thought about the flask and his half-empty coffee cup. He took a large swallow and felt the warmth again. He waited for Lake to continue.

"I was seeing this broad, you know. Cute chick, but a flirt. She came on to Andy, and I didn't think nothin' of it. She flirted with everybody. Next thing I know, they went away for the weekend together. Old Andy and I had it out and never had much to do with each other after that. Then we ended up both living in the Village. I wasn't glad about that at first, but we started hanging out together again. I decided that broad was in the past. We became friends again … at least for a while," he added.

"When did you last see Burgess?"

"It's been a while. I dunno, maybe a few weeks. I don't remember."

"Where did you see him last?"

"*Didn't I just say I don't remember?*" Lake shouted, jumping up from his chair. Within seconds, Gabriel was by Lake's side, and the officer in the hall was at his other side. Lake sat. "Sorry," he mumbled. "I got this temper here. Sorry."

"Well, I can see you have a temper, Mr. Lake. Where were you the night Mr. Burgess was killed?"

"I dunno. Prob'ly out drinkin'. That's where I usually am."

"So, back to this temper of yours. I'm wondering just how you took it when you learned that your wife was seeing Mr. Burgess." Shields stared directly at Lake while the other two officers closed in, ready to respond to any sudden movement Lake might make. But to the surprise of all three men, Lake just dropped his head and muttered a response.

"Sorry, Mr. Lake. I didn't hear that. Tell me what happened when you learned about the affair."

"There was no affair. Andy and I worked it out." Lake's head still hung low, and he looked defeated.

"Exactly *how* did you work it out, Mr. Lake? By killing him, perhaps?"

Gabriel knew Shields couldn't keep taunting Lake without causing him to lose his temper. He wondered if he was doing it intentionally. Suddenly, and to Detective Gabriel's surprise, Shields said, "That will be all for today. We will be talking to you again. Stay in town." Detective Shields walked out of the room. Gabriel and the officer looked at each other, both clearly puzzled, but they tried not to let it show.

"Let's go, Mr. Lake." Gabriel and the officer accompanied Lake to the elevator and down to the first-floor exit. Lake walked off with his head down and his hands deep in his pockets. He turned into the bar two doors down.

"What was that all about?" Gabriel asked Shields when he returned.

"I wanted to check some things out before we did any more questioning of Lake. I didn't want to have to read the guy his Miranda rights just yet."

In fact, Shields knew his own temper was escalating, and he was losing his edge in the interrogation. The Department had nothing on Lake other than a possible motive. There was no other evidence.

And Shields needed a drink.

Chapter 19

There was some unexpected excitement at Sarah's next quilt class. Frank came in waving his arms and anxiously announcing that he had a serious problem. Once the class calmed him down, he sat at the table, and, somewhat less agitated, explained that he had just learned there had been a murder in Cunningham Village. He said they lived very close to the Village and he had a friend who lived there. The friend told him about the murder.

"The dead guy's name was Andy, and my friend knew him," he added. "Do you think my grandma and I are safe?" he asked excitedly. "My granddad died, and it's my job to keep us both safe."

Ruth immediately consoled him, saying, "Frank, you're safe, and so is your grandmother. Whoever did this is certainly long gone by now, and if not, the police will catch him. You don't have a thing to worry about."

Frank seemed somewhat pacified by her answer and reluctantly turned his attention to his fabrics. The subject was apparently dropped as the group began comparing their fabric choices and admiring the completed table runner Ruth had put on the design wall.

"He even knows who did it," Frank added so quietly it was little more than a whisper.

Sarah wasn't sure what she had heard. She moved to the chair next to Frank and said very quietly and calmly, "What did you just say, Frank?"

"My friend knows who did it," he repeated quietly. "It's a secret. I wasn't supposed to tell that part."

"Have you spoken to the police?" Sarah asked.

It was immediately evident that was the wrong thing to say. Frank had what many young mothers refer to as a meltdown. He began crying and rocking back and forth in his chair. Again, Ruth was able to calm him, and Sarah assured him it was still a secret. "Let's just work on our quilts and forget all this scary stuff," Ruth said. "Okay, Frank? Shall we sew a beautiful little quilt for your grandmother?"

"Yes," he said reluctantly, and within a few minutes, he was eagerly showing off the fabrics he had chosen. He had an old-fashioned rose pattern in pale peach for the border and a companion fabric with the tiniest of rose buds. His other fabrics were perfectly coordinated, reflecting Ruth's influence.

Sarah followed along with the class and was able to keep up with all the instructions and new skills. But a part of her mind was playing back what Frank had said. She wondered how she could find out more. She wondered how much the grandmother might know and how she could find out without causing Frank more anxiety. She wondered if it was fear he felt or simply that he didn't want to betray his friend.

When she got home that night, she called Sophie. "May I come over?" she asked. Sophie, as always, was delighted to have company, and when Sarah arrived, there was already a plate of cheese and crackers on the coffee table, two glasses, and a bottle of wine, opened and ready to pour.

"Let's have a party," Sophie announced as Sarah came in.

"Well, Sophie, I didn't come with a party in mind, but now that you mention it, it's exactly what I need."

The two women relaxed for a while and enjoyed the refreshments. Sophie had already added a sizzling pan of chicken wings and several sauces, and, of course, a plate of her famous peanut butter cookies.

"I didn't expect a feast," Sarah said lightly, "especially since I invited myself."

"Well, I happen to know you didn't have dinner before your class, and we can enjoy this little feast and still deal with whatever is on your mind tonight. And don't try to deny it. I can see it in your eyes. Speak up, friend. What's going on?"

Sarah told Sophie about the quilt class and what Frank had shared. She admitted she was completely at a loss as to how to deal with this new information. "I hesitate to go to Detective Shields. You know how he is, and he'd send Frank into a coma. And I hesitate to go to the grandmother. I just don't know what to do … and do you think if Frank really knows something, he might be in some danger?"

"Hmm. Let me think about this," Sophie said somewhat unclearly due to the chicken wing she held between her teeth just ready to strip off the meat.

They sat thinking for awhile, and finally Sophie spoke up saying, "I believe that we have to investigate this quietly and on our own. Frank knows you and must have had some level of trust because he did tell you. I think we need to use you to get more information from him, and we need to develop a strategy that will keep Frank from getting upset."

"We can work on the strategy. It will probably have to have something to do with quilting since that's about all Frank and I have in common," Sarah offered.

"How about this," Sophie proposes. "Let's sit here and relax, enjoy our snacks, and talk about pleasant subjects. You can tell me what you're doing in your quilt class, and I'll tell you about the hilarious Mahjong game at the center this morning. Tomorrow we'll figure out what to do because, as Scarlett has assured us all, 'Tomorrow is another day.'" She cackled all the way to the kitchen and returned with another plate of chicken wings.

Chapter 20

Sarah spread out her squares on the kitchen table and admired them as she sipped her coffee. Ruth had told her she had done an excellent job with her star points and that her seam allowances were perfect. She was feeling much more confident about quilting and was thinking that she just might be able to do that tie quilt after all.

But first, she thought, she wanted to make a floral quilt for her couch. Her own garden was growing beautifully, but it didn't bring her the joy that her secret garden had at home. It surprised her that she still thought of her little cottage in Kings Valley as home. She moved to the back patio and looked at the little garden square that was now filled with a rainbow of color. "Thank you, Andy," she said to the wind. "Thank you for my garden."

After breakfast, Sarah dressed for her day out. She was feeling nervous about meeting the retired policeman. She had never done any volunteer work and wasn't exactly sure what would be expected. Marjory had said, "It's easy. Just be a friend. Listen. Talk. If Charles wants, you might even take a walk together. I'd love to see him get out of that house once in a while. I'm glad he agreed to come to the center to meet you at the coffee shop. He has really isolated himself."

* * * * *

A lovely trim woman stepped somewhat timidly into the coffee shop and looked around. She wore a soft pastel dress and carried a shopping bag with a needle and thread logo. Her curly blond hair was cropped just below her ears and was tinged with gray. *She was a beautiful woman*, he thought, *and she still is.*

"Are you Charles?" she asked, approaching his table.

"Yes, I am. Charles Parker." He stood and shook her hand. It felt soft, yet strong.

"My name is Sarah," she said smiling. "May I sit down?"

It's her eyes, he thought. *There's something in those eyes that has haunted me for years. I wonder if she'll remember me.*

"Charles Parker," she repeated his name slowly. "They gave me your name at the center. But now that I see you, I feel we've met before."

He so wished he didn't have to remind her of that day—that terrible day. He did not respond.

They ordered coffee and sweet rolls and chatted about this and that. They were both a bit uncomfortable, as strangers often are. She told him about some of her activities that she called her new hobbies—quilting and the computer. They talked about some of the activities available in the Village. He told her about his woodworking and said, "I just make small things: birdhouses, small boxes, things like that." They came up with a couple of activities they might enjoy doing together.

"So you go by Charles, not Charlie?" She asked.

"I was Charlie on the job, but since I retired, I've been introducing myself as Charles. My wife always called me Charles, and I like that best. Some people even shorten it to Chuck, which I don't like at all," he responded with a smile.

"Well then, I'll call you Charles. Tell me about your family. How many children do you have?" She purposely didn't ask about his wife since she knew that could lead them both down a depressing path.

He told her about his sons who were living in Colorado, but without much detail. She told him about Martha and Jason. As they talked, they became more comfortable with each other and began making plans for future get-togethers.

"There's no reason our visits have to be confined to the coffee shop," Sarah suggested. "The day trips on the Village bus have always sounded like they would be fun. Last month they went to a century-old mansion with acres and acres of amazing gardens. They walked through the gardens and had a tour of the house. There was even a tea room where the group had lunch. Is that something you might like to do?"

"I guess so," he responded. "I've never thought about it. I don't go out much. I don't know anyone, and everyone seems to have their own friends."

"Well, since I've been here," Sarah offered, "I've learned you just have to talk to whomever is willing to listen. Just last week, I …"Sarah stopped in the middle of her sentence. Both eyebrows shot up as she looked directly at him.

"Wait," she exclaimed. "Wait a minute. Charles Parker? Retired policeman? No wonder you look so familiar to me. You're that kind officer who told me about Jon."

Charles lowered his head, feeling embarrassed, and said, "That was so many years ago. I'm surprised you remember."

"Remember? I could never forget your kindness that day. And your phone call when my grandson died. You are a very kind man. I'm so glad we've met again." Sarah felt an unfamiliar excitement as they sat and drank their coffee. "Of course, I'm not sure I should be assigned to you as your friendly visitor since we know each other already. I'll ask Vicky tomorrow. But that doesn't mean we can't be friends and take those bus rides. We might even find a class at the center we would both enjoy."

What's this excitement I'm feeling? And at my age! Get a grip, Sarah.

* * * * *

The next day, Vicky agreed that it was problematic for Sarah to be the official friendly visitor for someone she knew prior to coming to the Village. Vicky had been uncomfortable about assigning her to a man in the first place. That was rarely done, but having far more women than men who were interested in volunteering, it was sometimes necessary.

After Vicky learned that they had discussed doing some activities together, she wondered if he would even need an official visitor. Perhaps Sarah, as a friend, could get him involved in the community. That was Vicky's goal in the first place. She felt Charles Parker was depressed and could benefit from some human contact.

She discussed it with both of them separately by phone, and both agreed. In fact, they had already arranged to meet at the center the next day to go over the class schedules and look in on some of the ongoing activities.

Chapter 21

Sarah arrived at her quilting class right on time. She only had two more classes and wondered how she would get the table runner finished in such a short time. At this point, she had her eight squares completed and eight strips of fabric cut for the inner and outer borders, but she could see there was a lot left to do before it would be a completed table runner.

She was surprised to find that, after just a half hour at the sewing machine, she had all the blocks sewn together and was beginning to attach the inner border. By the end of the class, she had her borders on and Ruth was lining up all the completed tops on the design board. It amazed everyone how different each table runner looked.

Sarah's appeared soft with its pretty pale pastels, and Frank's was very old-fashioned looking, almost as if it were an antique already. The two young mothers had used very modern fabrics: one was done in black and white with just a touch of red, and the other one was done in batiks. Ruth carried an incredible line of batiks in dazzling colors and patterns. Sarah was tempted to buy a few pieces but was trying to hold off until she knew how she would use them.

Ladies in the Quilt Club had talked about their *stash* and how they were sorry they had bought fabric simply because they liked it. Now they had bins and closets and drawers full of fabric, and still, when they did a project, they turned to Stitches and not to their stash. "Buying the fabric is the best part," one quilter had said with a chuckle.

Sarah started thinking about where she would keep her stash if, in fact, she started accumulating fabric. She thought about the guest room that was decorated with furniture left over from the kids. Nothing really matched, and no one ever visited anyway. *Maybe, just maybe, that could be a quilting room.*

After class, Sarah walked quickly up the street to catch up with Frank. "Hi, Frank," she said a bit out of breath. "I love your grandmother's table runner."

"My little quilt? Yes, I like it, too. But I wonder if I should have made it with the fabrics like the one in the window. That's the one she liked."

"Oh, Frank, she'll love the one you're making. Grandmothers love anything made by the kids, and actually, I think yours is very similar to that one." They had reached the corner and were directly across from Dave's Diner. "Hey, you know, I'm starving," Sarah exclaimed. "How about you? Do you want to grab some lunch at the diner?"

Frank hesitated and looked around sheepishly. "I don't know, Miss Miller ... I don't usually eat out ..."

Thinking that perhaps he didn't have the money, Sarah added, "Oh please. I want to treat you to lunch. I really hate to eat alone, and I'm very hungry." She hoped to spend some time with him and begin to gain his trust. Maybe he would share more information with her—if not today, then soon.

She knew that whatever information he had should go to the police, but she was reluctant to turn the belligerent Detective Shields loose on the young man.

"Well, okay. I could do that. I'm very hungry, too," Frank confessed. And hungry he was. He devoured a triple burger and a huge order of fries, washing it all down with a chocolate shake. As they ate, they talked about quilting, his time at the workshop, and his job at Keller's Market. She asked if he had lots of friends and he said he did, but then he started talking about his quilt again.

After their lunch, as they were leaving the diner, Sarah said, "You mentioned living near Cunningham Village. Did you walk here?"

"Yes, it's not far. I take the bus most places, though."

"Would you like a ride home? I brought my car today." Actually, Sarah brought her car specifically so she could offer Frank a ride home. She didn't want to involve the grandmother if it could be avoided. But she thought it might be helpful, at least, to know where he lived in case it became necessary to pass any of the information on to the investigators.

"Sure. That would be great," Frank responded. "It's not far. Just up the road. My grandma and I walk down here to the store all the time."

"Your grandmother sounds like a very special person. I'm glad you're making her such a beautiful gift."

"I leave it at the shop. If I take it home, I'm afraid I'll get excited and show it to her. I want it to be a big surprise on her birthday," he said. His whole face beamed with anticipation.

"Stop here," he said abruptly. "That's grandma's house right there." He pointed to a large Victorian house painted in purple and pale green. "That's my room up there on the top," he said pointing to a dormer window protruding from the third floor. A woman, older than Sarah had pictured, was sitting on the porch knitting. She waved to Frank and looked with curiosity at the car. Sarah waved back and told Frank to let her grandmother know who drove him home so she wouldn't worry.

"See you Friday at the library," he hollered to her as he approached the house.

At the library? Then she got it. Frank hadn't told his grandmother about the class. Driving home, she couldn't help but wonder about Frank's grandmother living in such a big house. Maybe there were other people there, but if not, that was a lot of house for a widow. Later, she wondered about how quickly Frank had come up with a cover story.

And even later, she wondered what Charles Parker was doing.

Chapter 22

Early the next morning, there was a loud banging at Sarah's front door. She rushed down and opened the door, leaving the security chain in place. "Sophie? What's going on?"

Once Sarah got the door opened, Sophie said excitedly, "Put the coffeepot on, kiddo, we've got business to conduct!"

"Business?" Sarah asked sleepily.

"You bet. Last night that imbecile Shields and his crew did a door-by-door search of everyone's house on the block. Well," she continued, "everyone who would let him in. He didn't have a search warrant, and I sure didn't let him into my house. He'll be here in an hour or so. He said he would come back to see everyone who wasn't home last night. Where were you, anyway?" Sophie asked.

"Sophie, you've given me so many things to respond to … and I haven't had my coffee, so let's move to the kitchen and slow this thing down." While she was starting the coffee, she said, "Let's start with where I was and get that out of the way. I was at the community center using the computer. I was looking up fabrics and quilt patterns, and the time got away from me." She set out mugs and stuck some sweet rolls in the oven to warm. She didn't mention that Charles Parker was there with her.

"You don't have time for all this quilting stuff, girl. We have a murder to solve."

"Okay, Sophie, let's look at this logically. First of all, Detective Shields told us to stay out of the investigation ..." Sarah began, but Sophie immediately interrupted her.

"... and you think that's going to cause us to stay out of it?" Sophie bellowed. "Andy was our friend, and going around looking in his neighbors' houses isn't going to solve his murder. I want to know what happened, and I want to know now."

"Okay, Sophie. Calm down. It's too early for hysterics. What is it you want to do?"

"I want to see the security tapes," Sophie responded.

"Why?"

"Because I don't think the police knew what to look for. I want you and me to go over to the security office and ask to see the tapes. And I don't want to ask for Shields's permission." Sophie's voice escalated as she talked and took on a tone that dared anyone to challenge her. "This is our community, and those security tapes belong to us. We pay for our security and we pay for those tapes, and we have the right to see them." Sophie sat up straight in the chair and looked as indignant as her round face, curly hair, and pink elephant pajamas would permit.

"No argument, Sophie. I agree. But I know what Shields will have to say if he finds out what we did."

"Not interested," Sophie said, dismissing Sarah's concerns. "I don't care what he has to say. I want to see the tapes."

"Okay, Sophie. Let's have some coffee …" as she removed the steaming hot pan from the oven, "… and some sweet buns and talk about how we will go about this."

Immediately after breakfast, Sarah showered and got dressed while Sophie did the same at her house. They agreed to meet at Sophie's house at 9:30 and walk over to the security office that was located next to the center. Although there was a community shuttle that circulated around the community providing transportation to and from the center, Sarah always preferred to walk. Sophie, on the other hand, was no fan of walking and complained all the way that they should have taken the bus. "We'll be too tired to view the tapes," she complained. Not one to tell other people what was good for them, Sarah often would trick Sophie into taking a healthier approach when she could. Sophie, she felt, certainly needed the exercise and fresh air. If asked, Sophie would have disagreed.

They had decided not to call ahead and ask if they could view the tapes. They didn't want to give the security folks the opportunity to say no. Instead, they entered the building cheerfully and simply said that they were there to view the tapes for the day of Andy's disappearance.

"I don't know if I'm allowed to show you those," Paul, the security guard on duty, said hesitantly. "We've never had anyone ask before."

"Well …" Sophie began, being as tactful as she could since Sarah told her to calm down and try to get on the good side of the staff, "… we just want to take a peek and see if we notice anything the police might have missed. We know the people here and just might see something that would help them."

"Oh, I didn't realize you were helping the police with this. Of course you can see the tapes," Paul said, leading them to the back office. Sarah and Sophie looked at each other with surprise but remained as expressionless as they could. Paul had misunderstood and thought they were working with the police. This helped them with being able to view the tapes but sure would not help them with Detective Shields.

"Leave it alone, kiddo," Sophie whispered as they followed Paul down the back hall. "We'll deal with the consequences later."

"You just want to see that day?" Paul asked.

"Yes," Sarah responded. "Just that day, and you can start in the late afternoon if you don't mind. We'll have to watch activity way into the night, and that could take many hours. Is there a way to speed it up?"

"The camera is motion activated, so it only comes on when someone approaches the gate," Paul offered. "It will go pretty quickly. We don't have a lot of traffic coming and going through the gates except on weekends."

It turned out to be a very dull day. Sophie and Sarah watched cars coming and going. Visitors stopped to identify themselves, and the guard occasionally called ahead to verify the visit. The speaker was controlled by the guard and was clicked on whenever he was speaking with visitors.

"Stop it here." Sophie demanded. "Isn't that Andy coming in? What's that car?"

"Just a minute," Paul said. "There's audio with this."

"Hi, Andy. What's with the new car?" the guard asked.

"Not new. I'm just test driving it for someone," he said rather abruptly. He wasn't his usual friendly self. The guard waved him through.

The tapes were a bit grainy, and the women couldn't tell if there was anyone else in the car.

"Whose car was he testing?" Sophie asked Sarah.

"I don't know anything about it," Sarah responded. "I saw Andy earlier in the afternoon, but he didn't mention anything about test driving a car. Does he know anything about cars?"

"How should I know?" Sophie responded impatiently. "What time was that?" she asked Paul.

"16:10," he responded, and Sophie frowned. "4:10 in the afternoon," he added.

"This car left again around 2:00 in the morning. Unfortunately, the driver had his face turned and sped through the gate. The police must not have been very interested in this car because they never talked to me about it. I've tried to find out how they're doing, but that Detective Shields treats me like I'm the killer."

"He treats us all like that, Paul. Don't take it personally."

A few hours later, they viewed the scene Paul had described. The white car sped through the gate without even slowing down, took an immediate right, and was instantly out of sight.

Sophie was livid. "How could Detective Shields tell us it had to be an inside job when he knew about this car? Obviously, this car belongs to the killer. He was murdered by whoever asked Andy to test drive the car. Someone must have seen the driver."

"If that was even the real reason he was driving the car. Maybe he wasn't test-driving it but had it for some other reason. At any rate, I agree with you that we may have just witnessed the flight of the killer," Sarah said. Turning to

Paul, she asked, "What did the police have to say about this scene?"

"Well, as I said, they never mentioned it. Then, just a couple of days ago, I called to ask about their progress and told him I was wondering about the white car. Detective Shields didn't tell me anything but asked me to send him a copy of that portion of the tape."

"Did you send it?"

"Yeah, I sent it, but I never heard a word back. When they're investigating here in the Village, it's like we don't exist. Heck, we know more about what goes on here than they ever will. Some of us were even on the force before we came here."

"Well, Paul," Sarah consoled. "I don't think it's the way they all feel. There are bad apples everywhere, and it seems we've run into one."

On their way home, they stopped at the coffee shop in the community center for an early dinner. They had missed lunch and were too tired to fix dinner at home.

At Sophie's insistence, they took the shuttle home. Sophie was quiet most of the way. As they exited the bus, she asked, "What do you think of all this, Sarah?"

"I don't know what to think, but I'm wondering now about what Millie told us. That afternoon he received a disturbing phone call and left their aerobics class. But I ran into him shortly after that, and he seemed okay. In fact, he told me he would bring his tie quilt by, and he did that."

"How was he when he came by?" Sophie asked.

"He seemed rushed and distracted. He wouldn't even come in. He just handed me the box and said he would see me next week. He wasn't his usual self."

"I'm stymied," Sophie said in a dejected tone that Sarah had never heard from her. "What in the world was Andy involved in?"

"I can't answer that, Sophie. But I will say that I totally trusted Andy. He was a good man, and despite the alleged affair with Millie, I still regard him as having been a valued friend and a good person. I know there's some explanation for all this."

After she got home, she decided to sit down with Charles the next day and talk to him about it. Even though he was retired, she felt he could help get all these scattered facts into one cohesive story that would make sense.

… And tomorrow is another day.

Chapter 23

The telephone was ringing as Sarah stood up. She had just planted two crimson star coneflowers in what she was beginning to call "Andy's Garden." She got inside just in time, wiping the wet soil from her hands on the dish towel hanging on the stove. "Hello," she answered.

"Mrs. Miller?" the voice asked.

"Yes, who's calling please?" She wished people would identify themselves when they called. Andy had told her about telephones that had caller ID, and she wished she had one. She brought her old phones with her when she moved to the Village, and it was certainly time to update them. "Get with the times, gal." Andy had said.

"This is Nancy from the animal shelter. How are you today?"

"I'm doing fine. I was just outside doing a little gardening."

"It's a beautiful day for that," Nancy responded. "I was calling you to check out something. I know you were looking for a dog that could provide protection as well as companionship when you came in last week."

"Yes," Sarah responded.

"Well, we brought in a young rottweiler yesterday. That's an excellent dog if you need protection. They become very attached to you and will protect you from anything."

"But a rottweiler …" Sarah said hesitantly.

"Well, there are a few issues I wanted to point out first. For one thing, he's not very big right now, but he can reach one hundred pounds or more."

"That's a lot of dog for me to handle. I'm nearly seventy, and I'm not sure I could manage a dog that big."

"Yes, I thought about that. Rex is a real sweetie and will make someone a great pet if they treat him right. I thought of you, I guess because I know you would be gentle with him and show him lots of love. He's already had a tough time in his short life. Rottweilers tend to be intelligent and easy to train. But he'll grow very large, and he'll become very attached to you."

Nancy continued, "The thing that perhaps concerns me is that rottweilers are one-person dogs—very territorial—and I suspect many of your friends are older folks since you live in Cunningham Village. He could possibly hurt someone unintentionally."

"Yes, you're right. I think we need to stick with a smaller dog. I could never hold a one hundred–pound dog back if he decided a friend of mine was a threat to me," Sarah said. "I'm not even sure, anymore, that protection is what I need. I started out wanting that, but as I thought about having a dog, I realized what fun it would be to have a furry friend to take walks with and to keep me company here at home."

"That's exactly what a dog can give you, plus that wonderful unconditional love. They're there for you no matter what," Nancy added.

"When I came to see you," Sarah continued, "we had just had a tragedy in the neighborhood, and I think I may have overreacted a bit. I don't really need protection. I'm perfectly safe here," Sarah added, wondering if that was at all true.

They agreed that Nancy would keep an eye out for the right dog and that Sarah would stop in from time to time to meet the ones that were there.

As she was falling asleep that night, Rex came to her mind. She mulled over the little she knew about him—that he's had a tough time in his short life—but she decided to remain steadfast in her resolve to not adopt a pet because she felt sorry for it. She would wait for the dog that was the right one for her. *I'll know it when I meet him.*

* * * * *

The next day, Sarah and Charles met at the center for coffee and then went to the Resource Room to get class schedules. On the way, she took him around to see the pool. He was interested in doing laps, and they found that there were times set aside specifically for lap swimming. He hadn't said much about his stroke but did say that his physical therapist would be pleased if he swam regularly. Sarah admitted that she had never learned to swim but thought she would enjoy the water aerobics class. "I've just filled my days to the point I can't find the time to do all of the things I'd like to do."

"What do you spend most of your time on?" Charles asked.

"Well, there's the quilting, but that doesn't really take much of my time yet. And there was the computer class that got me onto the computer and onto the internet. I go to the lab several times a week and write emails and look up things I'm interested in. That has opened a whole new world for me. I think about buying a computer to have at home, but there's something about coming here to see people and socialize. Social contact is important as we get older."

"I think you've been talking to Vicky," Charles said with a knowing smile. "That's exactly what she says I need."

"It's exactly what we all need." Sarah responded, also with a smile. "The more I think about it," she continued, "I guess most of my time is spent with Sophie and some of the other people on our block trying to piece together what might have happened to our good friend, Andy."

"Andy? That would be Andy Burgess, the guy who was killed here, right? You knew him?"

"Not only did I know him but he was also one of my good friends. Andy got me into computers. He and Sophie, who lives across the street from me, were instrumental in getting me acclimated to life in the Village. They introduced me to people and showed me the ropes. I was a real sad sack when I came here—at least that's what Sophie told me the day we met. I'd left my home and the life I knew and moved into what felt like a whole new world. I'll always have a special place in my heart for all the help those two gave me."

"It must have been very hard for you when Burgess died," Charles said sympathetically.

"Well, you certainly saw me at a much worse time, but it has been hard. And because of the connection we all had, Sophie and I have tried to find out what happened to him."

"Have you talked to the police about it?" Charles asked.

"They've talked to us about it, but they don't seem to want to share much information with us. In fact, we've been reprimanded a time or two for sticking our noses in where they weren't welcomed."

Charles laughed a deep hearty laugh. "I know what you mean. We cops can be very territorial." Sarah hadn't heard him laugh before and was surprised at how his face lit up. His eyes were twinkling and she thought, not for the first time, that he was a very handsome man.

"Funny," she said. "That's the second time I heard the word territorial this morning."

"… and the first?" he asked.

"It was said in reference to a rottweiler."

Again, he laughed and said, "Well, there are many similarities there."

I like this man. I really like this man.

They walked on to the Resource Room and picked up the current class schedule. Charles said he would go over it and promised to pick out one class. "I already have a few ideas about what I might enjoy," he said. "One is the woodworking class …"

"But you already know woodworking …"

"Yes, yes, I know, but it would be a way to meet some guys that are into it, too, and you're the one encouraging me to get to know some people."

"You'll be teaching the class before long, I suspect," Sarah said teasingly. "Shall we get some lunch?"

"Let's celebrate and have a fancy lunch in the restaurant. Are you game?" he asked.

"Okay, but we go Dutch treat, and you tell me what we are celebrating."

"We're celebrating a new chapter in our lives." He guided her into the dining room with his hand gently on her back.

His touch brought a slight shiver to her spine that she felt but hoped he didn't notice.

Across the room, she spotted Sophie and her gang of cohorts. Sophie's boisterous voice could be heard throughout the room. "Hey, kiddo. Get over here with us where you belong."

She turned to Charles and, hoping she wasn't being presumptuous and perhaps a bit forward, said, "Let's eat alone. I'd really like to talk to you more. Okay?"

"It's more than okay with me, but go speak to your friends. I'll get us a table."

Sarah crossed the room, realizing that she just might be slightly blushing. She greeted everyone and said, "I'd love to join you, but Mr. Parker and I have some business to discuss." To Sophie, she said, "I'll see you back home later. Okay?"

"Hmm. They have 'some business to discuss,'" Sophie said somewhat suspiciously. "Interesting. And just imagine having business to discuss with such a handsome man." The women at the table giggled and Sarah's blush deepened.

"It's not like that, Sophie," she objected. "He's a friend, and we just need to catch up."

"Well, you get your hiney over to my house the minute you get home. You have some explaining to do." Sophie then burst into her contagious cackle that could be heard throughout the dining room.

Much to Sarah's surprise, Sophie and her group gave them their privacy, and she and Charles spent an incredible two hours enjoying white wine, a delicious seafood pasta, and light conversation. They were having such a good time that Sarah decided not to approach the topic of Andy today.

She did want to talk to him about it, but not while they were having so much fun.

Back home, Sarah remembered Sophie's demand that she report to Sophie's house and explain herself. But she felt too good to do that. Instead, she decided to sit down at her window and thumb through her *Introduction to Quilting* book and think about the lovely day she had had with the very interesting Charles Parker.

Sophie can just wait. I want to enjoy this new feeling.

Chapter 24

His face was red and his fists were clenched. "Do you women realize you can be arrested for obstruction of justice?" Detective Shields shouted.

"Have we done something to annoy you, Detective Shields?" Sophie asked with wide, innocent eyes.

"Annoy me? *Annoy me?* You've gone too far this time, ladies. You had no right to view those tapes and come in here asking me to account for my actions, or 'lack of actions,' as you put it." Sarah noticed his hands were shaking as he downed an entire mug of coffee in one large gulp.

"Look," Sarah began in a soft voice, hoping it would help to lower the volume in the room. "We're all on the same side, aren't we? We want to know who killed Andy. I guess we have different reasons, but our goal is the same. Why are you so upset with us about this?"

"I owe you no explanation," Shields shouted, "and I'm seriously considering letting you both cool your heels in jail tonight. I have obstruction. I have impeding an investigation. I might even have you on accessory to a murder."

"*What?*" Sophie screamed. "How dare you talk to us like this!" Sarah noted that the volume in the room hadn't, in fact, been lowered. She expected the pictures to fall off the wall soon.

Sophie stood and theatrically tossed one end of her scarf across the opposite shoulder. "We're out of here. If you plan to arrest us, you'd better do it right now." She headed for the door. Sarah was hesitant but gave Detective Shields a polite nod and followed her friend. They both expected him to follow right behind and slap handcuffs on them. But the hallway was quiet, and they progressed to the elevator without incident. As the elevator door opened on the first floor, they again expected to be met by police officers, but they were not. They headed for the front door and exited.

"I guess the SWAT team will meet us at the house," Sophie said sarcastically.

Shields slid his bottom desk drawer open and removed the flask. It was empty. He walked across the room to his briefcase and removed an unopened bottle of whiskey. Back at his desk, he filled the coffee cup and placed the bottle in the desk drawer. "No coffee this time, big guy?" he asked himself rhetorically.

As he sipped his second cup, he reflected on his morning. The sun had been shining when he left the house, and he had decided to walk to work. The fresh air always helped him clear his head after the early morning hysterics he had to listen to from the time the alarm went off until he could get out of the house. "Margaret would be drinking, too, if she had my job," he had muttered to himself. "I wish she would stop threatening and just go ahead and get out. Who needs this hassle?"

He refilled his mug and started reading the reports on his desk.

Sophie and Sarah were both shaking when they got into Sarah's car. "You put up a good front, Sophie, but I can tell that upset you."

"Me? When do I ever get upset? That *civil servant* can't upset me. He doesn't seem to realize he's here to serve us, not the other way around." Sophie huffed and puffed and continued to mutter, "He had no right to speak to us like that."

"Well, Sophie, I'm not sure we went about it in the right way." Sarah carefully chose her words. "You remember, we agreed to ask him about the white car and ask about the department's progress in locating it. We agreed to be calm."

"Yes, we agreed to that," Sophie said defiantly. "And that's exactly what we did."

"Well, Sophie, I think bursting into his office without knocking and demanding, 'What the Sam Hill is going on here?' just might have rubbed him the wrong way."

"Hmm. Well, I was angry."

"Yes, you were angry. So was I. But I don't think we made any progress in finding out what they're doing about the white car." They continued home and decided to go to Sarah's house for brunch. Neither had eaten that morning, as they had been very eager to talk to Detective Shields.

* * * * *

Shields set the reports aside. He went across the hall to the men's room and washed out his coffee mug. He had hoped no one would find out about the white car. They had lost several days due to his stupidity. His team had been viewing the security tapes for the days preceding the Burgess murder, and he decided to take over and personally view the tapes covering the night of the murder. As usual, he had stopped at the bar on his way to the security office and didn't arrive until nearly midnight.

He had been watching for several hours when he suddenly woke up with a start when the security guard came into the viewing room. He didn't immediately know how much he had missed. The guard had said, "It's 4:00 a.m., and you wanted to leave about now. Did you catch anything good?"

"Nah," Shields had replied, having no idea what he had missed. "Nothing that will help us anyway."

Several days later, the same security guard had called him. "I was wondering what you thought about that white car. I was just reviewing those tapes, and that car just flew by. I talked to Bud, the guy that was on duty that night. Bud didn't seem to know a thing about it, so I'm suspecting he was off doing something he shouldn't have been doing. He's on suspension because of it. You didn't mention it at the time, so I was just wondering …"

Shields interrupted, "The department is keeping that under wraps for now, so don't mention it to anyone else. I was going to call you today about it. I want a copy of that portion of the tape for the department. Send it over right away." Shields wondered if he would be able to cover his tail. *What white car?* he had wanted to ask.

Once the tapes arrived, he immediately went to work. The car left the community and turned right onto Honeysuckle. There was an entrance to the interstate a few miles up, and most likely that was where it headed. *North? South?* He had no idea, but he assigned officers to check with gas station and highway cameras in both directions. There were three white cars that fit the general description traveling south and another four traveling north at about the right time. They were able to trace five of the plates, and they were cleared immediately. On the other two, both traveling south, the plates were not clear enough to read. He didn't have the manpower to follow up with all the camera footage that would have to be reviewed. He had to wait and hope the killer made a mistake and hope his bosses never noticed the one he made.

It was an easy mistake to make, he assured himself. *It was late, and I was tired.* He vowed to stop beating himself up over it and pulled out the Burgess file. He went over the fingerprint reports, looking for something else he might have missed. Andy's prints were everywhere, of course. It was his home. Unidentified prints were found as well. And there were places where all the prints had been wiped clean. *Strange*, he thought. All the closet doorknobs were clean, as were all the handles on the dresser and cupboards. *Had the killer been searching for something? Did he find it?* Shields wondered.

He called Detective Gabriel into his office. They discussed the case for a while and decided to do a second search of the house. "Let's do this one ourselves," Shields said. They called their forensic unit and requested a technician to accompany them.

Upon arriving at Andy's house, they saw that the crime scene tape was still attached. "I thought we were taking this down so the sister could come get his stuff," Shields said.

"She isn't coming for several months, so we left it in case we needed to go over the place again. I'm glad now that we did. The place should be just like it was when the body was found." Sure enough, the place was a mess: drawers pulled out and dumped on the floor, closet contents thrown around, mattresses tossed aside. The chalk outline of the body was still there, and there was dried blood on the corner of the nearby table. "Looks like he hit his head here," Gabriel said.

"The guy took quite a beating before he went down, but the coroner confirmed that he died from the head wound. I wonder how the other guy looked."

Gabriel continued to look around the area where the body had been. "Yeah, I wonder. The coroner's report said this guy had defensive wounds. It must have been some brawl."

Confirming that there apparently was nothing the previous investigators had missed, the two detectives locked up and removed the crime scene tape. "It's been long enough," Detective Gabriel said. "Let's get this out of here so these people don't have to keep looking at it."

Once they got outside the Village, Detective Shields turned to Gabriel and asked, "You got time to stop for a drink?"

"Sorry, Mark. The kids have a play at their school tonight. Gotta get home. Sorry."

Shields drove Gabriel to his car at headquarters and continued down the street to Barney's. Once inside, he took his usual stool at the bar. "Hey Barney. How about a shot over here." The music played, the cobwebs in his head began to fall away, and the warmth of the alcohol gave him a feeling of mellowness that he couldn't get anywhere else.

At 1:00 a.m., Mark Shields opened his front door and entered as quietly as possible. He turned the light on in the foyer. The beam of light stretched across the floor, into the living room, and across his wife's angry face.

"Turn right around and get out!" she yelled. "*Now!*"

He opened his mouth to argue, but no words came. He staggered toward the door, falling against the wall. "Please, Margaret," he slurred. "Just let me sleep. We'll talk … later …"

"*Out!*" she shrieked. "*Out now.*"

He reached for the doorknob, opened the door, and tripped over a flower pot on the front porch. He landed head first on the edge of the first step, tumbled to the bottom, and lay unconscious, leaving a trail of blood behind.

Chapter 25

Nancy from the animal shelter sounded very chipper when Sarah answered the phone. "I think we may have found the perfect dog for you, Mrs. Miller," she said with enthusiasm.

"What kind is it?" Sarah asked apprehensively.

"Well, he isn't exactly any identifiable breed. I would say he's a mix of maybe a … oh, I really don't know what to tell you. He's medium sized, maybe twenty-five pounds, has brown curly hair, and is very friendly. He seems to know a few commands, so he probably had a home at one time. We picked him up eating out of a trash can behind Barney's Bar & Grill."

"He must belong to somebody," Sarah responded.

"Yeah, that's what we thought too, but no one has claimed him, and he didn't have a collar. I will admit, he's not real pretty, but he's a real sweetheart. I'd love for you to see him. This fellow deserves to have a home."

Sarah had intended to call Detective Shields first thing that morning and apologize for their behavior the day before—actually for Sophie's behavior, but she would accept half the responsibility. Maybe she would call him first and then drive by the animal shelter. She was a little nervous about calling, not knowing how he would respond. He seemed to be a man of few moods, mostly bad ones.

The phone rang again, and Sarah answered, reminding herself to get a phone with caller ID. "Hello?" she answered.

"Sophie here. What are you up today?" Sarah didn't want to mention her intention to call Detective Shields, but she told her about the call from the animal shelter.

"A dog?" Sophie exclaimed. "And what do you need with a dog? They're just a lot of trouble." Sarah attempted to explain but realized she couldn't explain the love for a pet to someone who didn't make that connection. Sophie grew up on a farm, and as she'd said many times, "Animals belong outside."

"Well, don't expect me to take care of that mutt when you're away," Sophie growled.

"And just how often have you known me to be away, Sophie?" Sarah responded in a teasing tone.

"You're right, kiddo. I should mind my own business, but you know me."

They arranged to have a cup of tea in the early evening at Sophie's house. As she hung up the phone, Sarah thought again about calling Detective Shields. His card was lying by the phone, so she dialed his number quickly before she lost her nerve.

"I'm sorry, Mrs. Miller. Detective Shields won't be in today."

"May I leave a message for him?"

"I'm sorry," she repeated. "I don't know when he'll be available. Can Detective Gabriel help you?"

"No, thank you. I'll call back." She hesitated, hoping the officer would give her some idea when he might be available, but there was no response. Sarah felt something was wrong, but clearly she was not going to get any more information.

Sarah dressed in jeans and a plaid flannel shirt over a tee-shirt. It was beginning to get cool, but it could warm up at any time. Autumn was appearing, but it wasn't promising to stay.

When she arrived at the animal shelter, Nancy led her back into the kennel she had visited before. She only recognized a couple of the dogs from that time. She hoped the others had been adopted. They passed the cage with the rottweiler, and Sarah knew she had made the right decision.

They turned down the next aisle of kennels, and there he was. Sarah caught her breath and placed her hand on her heart when she saw him. "Oh my!" she exclaimed. He had big brown eyes, almost the exact color of his coat. He was ever so slightly cross-eyed when he looked at her, but that just made her fall in love with him. He had a long snout of a nose and rather long whiskers that twitched when he opened his mouth. He was undoubtedly the straggliest dog Sarah had ever seen, but he was most certainly smiling at her. She smiled back, and he wagged his tail.

A handwritten sign was clipped to the cage: Barney. Barney was the perfect name for this homely hound mix. "We don't know what his name is. He had no tags. We named him Barney since that's where we found him—out behind Barney's Bar & Grill, but you can change that if you want." Nancy said. "He won't mind."

Nancy clipped a sturdy leash to his collar and said, "Come, Barney." Barney stepped out of the cage and trotted up the aisle beside her, head held high. Nancy led them out to the run and showed Sarah some of his tricks. "He appears to be a very smart fellow," Nancy said. "Someone has obviously trained him to sit, stay, and behave well on a leash."

Sarah looked at his short wagging tail, his sturdy build, and his straggly coat, and she smiled again. He looked back at her with appreciation and smiled back. They had made an instant connection. She had to have him. He had to have her.

Sarah and Nancy agreed that she could pick him up the next day. He had one more appointment with their vet to complete his shots. He had been neutered the previous week. Sarah wondered who would have let this wonderful dog go. She could hardly wait to take him home. As she was leaving, she wished he were going with her today.

Once Sarah got in the car to head home, she suddenly realized how much she had to do to get ready for his arrival. "He'll need a bed and a blanket, and dishes for food and water. Oh, and food," she said to herself aloud. "I'll have to call Nancy to see what he eats." But then she realized that he probably ate whatever they gave him in the kennel, and she decided to stop at the new pet store up the street from Stitches and ask them about food. "Treats. He'll need treats, too. Oh, and toys …"

"What have I gotten myself into?" she muttered.

But she smiled as she drove, feeling excited about having another love in her life. "*Another* love?" she exclaimed aloud. "Now where did that come from?"

Having completed all the preparations for Barney's arrival, she realized it was time to go to Sophie's house. She decided not to eat dinner since she knew, from experience, that the snacks Sophie would provide would more than fill her up.

* * * * *

"Hi, kiddo," Sophie greeted. "How was dog shopping?"

"Well, I have a new member of my family. His name is Barney. Now, I know you'll try not to like him … but, believe me, within five minutes you'll be in love."

"In love, huh? We'll see," Sophie grumbled. The coffee table was overflowing with cheeses, crackers of all types, biscuits and jam, hot chicken wings, and a bottle of chardonnay.

"Glad I didn't eat dinner," Sarah laughed.

"Surely by now you know you'll receive a handsome feast when you come to my house."

"Well, don't expect the same when you come to my house. I'm a plain, simple cook and certainly not the fanciest of hostesses."

"We'll see if that's true once you start bringing that good-looking man of yours to the house," Sophie responded.

"Good-looking man? What do you mean?" Sarah asked innocently. Sophie doubted the sincerity of the innocent look when she saw a smile attempting to spread itself across Sarah's face.

"Humph."

"Okay, okay," Sarah conceded. "I know you're talking about my new friend, Charles. He's a really nice man, and we've only had two or three visits together."

"You mean dates, right?"

"No. I don't mean dates. We just meet at the coffee shop or the dining room, walk around the community, or sit in the park. We talk and laugh. We just have fun," Sarah explained.

"Yes," Sophie responded. "That's what I said. Dates."

Sarah let out an exasperated sigh followed by a little smile. The two friends went on to other topics and had a delightful evening together. They were indeed becoming fast friends.

Chapter 26

Mark Shields opened his eyes slowly, trying to figure out where he was. This was a familiar feeling, waking up feeling disoriented, but usually he could identify his surroundings and, shortly after that, reconstruct why he was there. This time was different. There was a gurgling machine next to him, tubes in both arms, a monitor of some sort, and a pain in his temple that defied any morning-after headache he had ever experienced. He looked around for Margaret. He had a momentary memory of seeing her in the hallway. "At home?" he asked himself. He fought to recapture the memory but nothing came.

A nurse came into the room and asked how he was feeling. "Confused," he admitted. "Why am I here? This is a hospital, right?"

"Yes, you're in Memorial Hospital. You fell and cut your forehead, banged yourself up pretty bad, and possibly had a concussion. We want you to continue to remain still and let us monitor your progress. You're doing fine, but I imagine you're experiencing a bit of pain."

"A *bit* of pain?" Shields responded sarcastically. "… and you're a medical person? Why are my ribs bandaged?" he demanded.

"We x-rayed your ribs. You have two broken ribs, and your entire trunk is sprained from the way you twisted when you fell. You'll need to keep the bandages on for a while."

"I fell?" he wondered. He didn't remember falling, but he probably shouldn't ask. He would ask Margaret when she came. "Where's my wife?" he demanded.

"I haven't seen your wife, Mr. Shields."

"That's *Detective* Shields," he corrected. "Why isn't she here?"

"Sorry," she said as she left the room, not answering his question.

He tried to reach the phone, but it was out of his reach. He looked across the room and saw his clothes. There was probably a cell phone in his pocket. He attempted to get up but was restrained. He pushed the call button, but no one appeared. He pushed it numerous times. Still no one. He was able to reach the water pitcher on the nightstand. He lifted it as high as the pain would permit and threw it against the wall. It shattered. Still, no one came. He pulled off the patches that led to the monitoring equipment and attempted to stand. They all came.

Moments later he fought the sedation that was being injected into his veins. He saw a white car rushing past. He saw Margaret screaming wordlessly. He floated into oblivion.

"I called his wife several times, Dr. Mellon. The first time she said she had no interest in his condition, and we would have to wait for him to be awake to find out about his insurance." Nurse Brier continued, "I called two or three more times and left messages, but she hasn't called back. I really don't expect to hear from her."

"She hasn't even been here?" Dr. Mellon asked incredulously.

"No. And from the way she sounded on the phone, I doubt that she'll be coming. She's one angry woman."

The nurse was right. Margaret spent the morning packing her clothes. She called a cab around noon and left for the airport. Before leaving town, she called a friend whose husband was a locksmith and requested that he change the locks and hold the keys for her. She had already spoken with her attorney and requested that he serve the divorce papers he had been holding. She told him she would be back in a month or so. She told her best friend, confidentially, that she would be at her mother's villa in the south of France. Margaret was going to have that long-needed rest and forget the dysfunctional, drunken leach, Mark Benjamin Shields.

Chapter 27

Sarah tried calling Detective Shields the next morning but got the same cryptic response from the officer answering the phone, so she decided to go ahead and talk to Detective Gabriel. As it turned out, he wasn't available either, but she was able to leave a message. An hour later, Detective Gabriel returned her call.

Sarah was actually relieved to speak with him. He had always been pleasant with her and never made her feel like a criminal. She didn't learn anything about Andy's case. He did tell her, however, that they were broadening the investigation beyond Cunningham Village. "You mean it was not necessarily someone here?" Sarah asked eagerly.

"Yes, ma'am."

"That's a relief. You can't imagine what it's like to be suspicious of your friends and neighbors." She asked about Detective Shields and was told he would be away for some time; Gabriel would be directing the investigation for now. She wondered what that was about but didn't ask.

Darrell Gabriel was a tall, slender officer, probably in his late thirties, with chiseled features. He never liked his first name and was always called Gabriel on the job and Gabe by his friends. He had moved to Middletown two years ago from New York where he had worked homicide for most of his career. With a young family and little time to spend with them, he had searched for a vacancy on a small town force. When he was contacted by Chief Walker of the Middletown Police Department, he immediately knew this was what he and his family needed.

Middletown didn't have a homicide unit, as such, and rarely had a homicide. He hoped to spend more time with his family, and in his job, he hoped to actually be of service to the community. On his first week, he had helped Tim from the fire department release a cat stuck in a storm drain. "This is more like it," he had said to himself that day with a smile.

He was pleased when the chief decided to partner him with Mark Shields. The two men got along well and had much in common. Shields had worked homicide in Boston for thirteen years and seemed to be enjoying the less hectic lifestyle of Middletown. Shields had moved to Middletown several years before when he married Margaret. Margaret's family founded the town in the 1800s and owned most of the businesses. Margaret enjoyed the benefits of old money and refused to leave the family mansion in Middletown. Mark got a job with the local police force despite Margaret's objections. She felt it was unseemly for him to hold such a position.

The two men worked well together and complemented one another's skills. Dividing up the workload was always congenial. But after the first few months, Gabriel began to notice the alcohol. At first, he had the fleeting feeling he smelled alcohol on Mark's breath in the morning, but he decided it was probably left over from the night before. He knew Mark always stopped for a drink or two on his way home. But as time passed, he noticed it was often stronger in the afternoon. Then there was the talk around the office. He always defended Shields, both to other officers and even to himself.

Three months ago, however, things became more complicated. His lieutenant questioned him about the reports. Being a loyal partner, he said he hadn't heard the rumors and had no misgivings about Shields. He went so far as to say he didn't think office gossip should be taken seriously.

Just before receiving the call from Sarah Miller, Detective Gabriel's boss had called him into his office and told him about Mark's accident. The lieutenant had actually said, "He fell down his own steps in a drunken stupor, according to his wife." Gabriel knew this drinking issue was going to be looked at more closely now. Shields's drinking had been much more evident recently, even on the job. Then there was the white car. Shields had told him he fell asleep during the viewing. He said Margaret had been sick and he had been up with her the night before. Gabriel did not believe Shields's story. The excuses were more frequent, and this time Shields had made a big mistake. They had probably missed the opportunity to catch the killer because of his negligence. Gabriel knew he couldn't continue to cover for his partner.

The lieutenant told Gabriel to continue working the Burgess case, which he had intended to do anyway. He pulled the file, reread all the statements, and reviewed the details of the crime. He read the work Shields had done to track the white car after discovering his mistake.

He read the notes about the alleged affair between Andy and Millie Lake. They had brought Ralph Lake in for an informal interview. Lake was an angry man and certainly seemed capable of murder. He didn't seem particularly disturbed when he was told about the affair. Obviously, he already knew. *Perhaps he had already handled it. He certainly had a motive*, Gabriel mused.

Lake's alibi had checked out. He was, in fact, at Barney's drinking that night, or at least that's what his friends said. *But then his friends could be lying for him.* The bartender that night was new and didn't know Lake that well. He said Lake had been in often, but he wasn't sure about that night.

"Lake is all we've got," Gabriel muttered to himself. He doubted they could make a case stick without a confession, and they weren't likely to get that.

Chapter 28

After getting off the phone with Detective Gabriel, Sarah poured herself another cup of coffee. She didn't need the stimulation; she already had butterflies in her stomach. Today was the day she would pick up Barney. "I hope he likes it here," she said to herself. The small backyard was fenced, and he'd have a nice place to play. She might need to put a small protective fence around her little flower garden in the spring in case he was a digger.

She had put Barney's fleece-lined bed and his toys in the guest room and had found a small store-bought quilt to put in the bed. "I'll make him his own quilt once I learn how," she said aloud excitedly. His water dish was sitting on a plastic place mat in one corner of the kitchen. His food was in the pantry, and his food dish was in the cupboard.

The young man at the pet store had suggested she feed him twice a day and not leave the food out all day. "If he doesn't eat it, just pick it up and give it to him at the next meal. He'll eat when he's hungry, and he'll learn the schedule." A big cookie jar with a dog's face painted on the front sat on the countertop and contained an assortment of dog treats of all shapes and sizes.

The salesman had warned her against overfeeding with treats. "These are nutritious treats," he had said, "but your dog will prefer them to his food, so just use them for training and that occasional special time." He suggested a book on dog care that explained how to integrate the new dog into the family and especially emphasized the reasons she needed to become the alpha dog. She giggled at the suggestion but seemed willing to read the book. The young salesman had watched her leave, wondering if his own mother would have such a spunky attitude at Sarah's age.

It was almost time to leave. The animal shelter was expecting her around noon, and she made one last inspection to confirm that the house was ready for her new roommate. She put on a sweater, grabbed her bag, and left the house.

Barney was waiting in the lobby when she arrived. He smiled his usual smile when he saw her and wagged his tail. Apparently, he knew she had come for him. Sarah signed the final papers and exchanged the kennel's worn collar and leash for Barney's new leather ensemble. He pranced out of the door by her side without a single glance back. He hopped into the backseat and lay down on the new fleece seat cover Sarah had installed. Sarah, glancing right and left to be sure the pet-store salesman was not lurking nearby, passed Barney a big, juicy beef treat. He smiled and wagged his tail.

Just before she arrived home, she decided, on a whim, to call Charles Parker. She hadn't used the cell phone Martha had given her but had programmed Charles's and Sophie's numbers in just for practice. She was glad now that she had.

"Hello there, pretty lady," he answered.

"You have that caller ID thingy, don't you?" she exclaimed. She made yet another mental note to get new phones.

"I wanted to let you know that I just picked up Barney, and I'm very near your house. Would you like to come down to the curb and meet him?"

"Absolutely," he responded enthusiastically. "I'll be right down."

Sarah rolled the windows down on the curbside, and Charles came up to the car. Barney looked at Sarah as if to get permission. "It's okay," Sarah said and introduced them. Barney approached the window cautiously and looked deep into Charles's eyes. Obviously, he liked what he saw. His tail began to wag as he stuck his nose out of the window and sniffed the hand Charles had offered palm down.

"Glad to meet you, young man. You don't know how lucky you are. You're going home with the world's prettiest lady." He glanced at Sarah, who was slightly blushing.

"You terrible man," she teased, "lying to a little dog. How about joining us at home for a bite to eat? I was too excited to eat breakfast, and here it is lunchtime and I'm starving." She felt it was a bit bold to invite him to her house, but with Barney as a chaperone, it should be fine.

"Sounds great. I need to lock up, and I'll walk on over. I need the exercise. I'll be there in twenty minutes. You won't starve before that, will you?"

"That works for me. I want to spend a few minutes showing Barney around his new home."

When they arrived, Barney followed her into the house reluctantly. She scratched his ear and said, "Come on, boy. It's okay. This is your new home." She led him across the living room and into the kitchen. She showed him his water bowl and got a treat out of his cookie jar. He took it from her hand but put it on the floor and looked around. "Okay, I guess you want the grand tour first. So you've seen the living room and kitchen. There's not much more to see. This is my room here, and over there is your room. Well, you might have to give it up temporarily if we ever have a guest; but mostly that's your room." He sniffed the doggie bed and looked at the toys. Sarah tossed a furry bunny a few feet away, and he lunged toward it and scooped it up. Holding it in his mouth, he looked at her mischievously.

"Can you bring it to me?" she asked with her hand out. He carried it over and dropped it at her feet. "Good dog," she praised. She knew then that someone had loved this dog. She wrapped her arms around his neck and patted his curly back. "Well, I'm the one who loves you now." He smiled and wagged his tail.

She had just taken him out to the backyard when Charles arrived. "Sorry to take so long," he called from the fence. He had walked around to the back. "I figured you were out here when you didn't answer the front door." Sarah unlatched the gate and let him in.

"Have a seat out here for a minute. I'm just introducing Barney to the backyard." Barney was busy sniffing everything in the yard. There was the brick-bordered garden of fall flowers, a row of freshly planted rose bushes along the fence, several older bushes that had probably been planted by the previous owner, and a bird bath that Barney could just reach. He treated himself to a few laps of sun-warmed water. He then went to the far corner of the yard, circled a few times, and claimed that area for his personal use.

"Do you know what kind of dog he is? He looks a little like the Irish terrier my sister had."

"I know exactly what he is—a wonderful mix of all the sweetest dogs there ever were," Sarah replied, realizing that she was just a bit biased already. "Let's see if he'll stay out here for a while to explore the yard while we fix our lunch. Would you like a glass of tea?"

"Sounds terrific. But don't go to any trouble with lunch. I eat like a bachelor—usually over the kitchen sink."

"Well, in my house you get to sit at the table," she teased.

Barney didn't want to stay in the yard alone; he obviously wanted to keep Sarah in sight. He got the treat from the floor and curled up in the corner of the kitchen. He put the treat down near his nose, sighed deeply, and closed his eyes.

"He's right at home," Charles said. "I like what you've done with the place. It's very homey."

"I'm looking forward to making it even homier with the quilts I'll be making. You are, in fact, looking at my very first endeavor."

"Here on the table?" Charles asked. "This is beautiful. You made this?"

"Yes, in the class I was telling you about. Next, I'll be making a quilt to use on my couch." The two friends spent the rest of the afternoon talking, sipping tea, sitting in the backyard with Barney, and ultimately taking a long walk. As they walked, Barney sniffed the sidewalk, carefully recording the way back home, as dogs tend to do.

As he was leaving, Charles reached over and gave Sarah a one-arm hug and a quick kiss on the cheek. He was smiling as he left. Sarah was smiling, too, as the telephone rang.

"You little hussy, you. I saw that kiss."

"Sophie, that's no way to begin a telephone conversation, and it was not really a kiss, just a friendly gesture."

"Hmm. We'll see how friendly this is. That man is smitten. You should have seen the smile on his face as he walked away from your house."

"Nonsense," Sarah responded gruffly while silently giggling to herself. *I feel like a teenager.*

Chapter 29

Mark Shields got out of the cab at his house, limping to the door using the cane the hospital sent home with him. He had asked the driver to wait. He wasn't sure of Margaret's mood since she hadn't been to the hospital. He was angry about that but told himself he would not fight with her today.

His key didn't fit the lock. He knocked but got no response, so he banged harder. Still nothing. He called from his cell phone and heard the phone inside ring. No answer. She wasn't home, but why didn't his key work? He tried again. He motioned for the cab driver to continue to wait, and he went around to the back. Everything was closed down tight, with the shades drawn. "What the hell is going on here?" He felt the anger rise throughout his body. His hands began to shake. He returned to the cab and, with a rage in his voice that even frightened the burly cab driver, demanded to be taken to Barney's Bar & Grill.

* * * * *

Sarah and Charles had met at the café in town. She told him she would like to discuss a few things about Andy's death. They ordered sandwiches and coffee, and while they waited, they chatted about what they had been doing and talked about Barney, who had made himself right at home. After eating, they ordered another cup of coffee, and Sarah looked serious. "I'm worried, Charles. I don't think the police have gotten anywhere with their investigation. I want to know what happened to Andy. He deserves that much. He was a good man."

She went on to tell him about Frank, the young man in her quilting class who said he had a friend who knew who killed Andy. She told him that she had hesitated to talk to the police about it. "Frank is very fragile, and Detective Shields could push him over the edge. But I think Detective Gabriel has taken over the case. I have no idea why, but I think perhaps I could talk to him about it."

"I think you should, Sarah. Every little bit helps in an investigation." Charles had heard about Gabriel from several of his buddies on the force. "He's a good man," Charles added. "I could go with you if you'd like."

"Oh, thank you, Charles. That would make me feel so much better. My experiences in that building have not been good, and I was nervous about going."

"Let's walk over there after lunch," Charles said. They finished their coffee and together walked the two blocks to the police station. He took her hand, and she felt like a teenager and just a little embarrassed that someone would see them. He dropped her hand as they approached the building, and he opened the door for her. "We would like to see Detective Gabriel," he said as they approached the officer at the desk.

"Is he expecting you?"

"No. We were just taking a chance that he might be available," Sarah said.

"Let me check." After taking their names, the officer went to a phone out of earshot and spoke briefly to someone. Turning to them, he said, "You can go on back. He's in the last office on the right." Sarah looked at Charles inquisitively.

"That's Detective Shield's office," she whispered as they walked toward the office. "I hope we aren't going to be talking to both of them." But when they reached the office, Detective Gabriel met them with a smile and led them into the office. Sarah introduced the two men, and they shook hands.

Gabriel looked pleased to meet Charles. "Detective Charlie Parker. You have quite a reputation in the department. It's great to meet the legend in person." Charles looked embarrassed and modestly said he couldn't believe anyone even remembered him. "You broke some big cases in this department. The boys still talk about you over at Barney's."

They all took their seats, and after a few minutes of small talk, Sarah turned to the subject of the investigation. "We've been wondering if any progress has been made in Andy Burgess case. Also, I wanted to discuss something with you."

"To be honest with you, we are nowhere. We have no viable leads, and no motives have been found. We're at a standstill. We're just hoping that someone walks in here and confesses, but that's not likely to happen," he added with a smile.

"Well, I suspected as much," Sarah responded. She noticed that Detective Gabriel had made no reference to Ralph Lake or Millie, and she decided not to mention them.

"So, that brings me to the second issue," Sarah continued. She told Gabriel about the quilt class when Frank expressed his concerns about a murder happening so close to his home. "A friend of his told him about it, but the piece I wanted to talk to you about is the fact that this friend told Frank that he knows who did it."

"And you didn't report this?" Gabriel asked, but not in an accusing way. "Why?"

"Well, I'll be honest with you," Sarah began apologetically. "Frank is limited, perhaps with a mild intellectual disability. And he's sensitive and somewhat fragile. I just couldn't subject him to Detective Shields's methods. I had hoped to get him to tell me more, but I haven't been able to get him to open up about it. Do you have any ideas how this can be handled?"

"Yes. Absolutely. I have the perfect solution. I've just been assigned an assistant, Amanda Holmes. Officer Holmes is a young woman who just joined the department. She doesn't have much experience with us yet, but before attending the academy, she was a grade school teacher out in Utah. I think she would be just the person to go talk to your young friend. She's especially skilled at developing trust with potential witnesses. Let me see where she is." Gabriel left the room. Sarah looked relieved. Withholding this information had been difficult for her.

A young female officer entered the room, followed by Detective Gabriel. "I would like to introduce you folks. Officer Holmes, this is Sarah Miller and her friend Detective Charles Parker, and," turning to Amanda, "this is Officer Amanda Holmes." Officer Holmes extended her hand to Sarah and Charles.

"Where are you assigned, Detective Parker?" she asked.

"What Gabe neglected to say is that I'm now retired. Just call me Charles."

"And I'm Sarah. We're both happy to meet you, officer."

"I'm glad to meet you both. Please call me Amanda. I think this operation of ours is somewhat under the table, so let's keep it informal."

"I told Amanda what we're hoping to do," Gabriel explained, "but I also told her it's not my plan to handle this officially, at least not until we get more information. I don't want to take the chance that other officers might get involved and question Frank on their own." Sarah read between the lines that Gabriel intended to make sure Mark Shields didn't get involved. She was relieved.

"I appreciate your discretion, Detective Gabriel."

Amanda Holmes took a seat next to Gabriel's desk. She was about thirty-two years old, Sarah thought. She was pretty with short brown hair and deep brown eyes that sparkled with anticipation. She clearly was pleased with her new job. "Where shall we start?" Sarah asked.

Amanda spoke up saying, "Well, I thought we would approach this like an undercover operation. I think uniforms would spook the young man, from what Gabe told me. Sarah, do you know where I might have an opportunity to meet him informally?"

"Yes," Sarah responded. "He works at Keller's Market on South Street and has been coming to the Friday night quilting group at Running Stitches. He lives with his grandmother near Cunningham Village, but that's probably not the best place to visit him."

"I agree," she said. "I've been doing some quilting myself. I wonder if I could come to that group on Friday night?"

"Sure," Sarah responded enthusiastically. "It's open to anyone, and we would love to have you. Frank is very comfortable and open in that group."

"Okay then. Let's keep this between us. The shop owner doesn't need to know what we're doing, does she?" Amanda asked.

"Absolutely not. She'll be happy to welcome a new face, and who knows? You just might want to keep coming," Sarah said with a hopeful smile.

After they had all left his office, Detective Gabriel thought about their plans. He had respect for Sarah's judgment and wanted to do all he could to protect Frank from Shields's style of interrogation. He had just as much respect for Amanda and her ability to get the information they needed.

He didn't know, at this point, whether Shields would occupy this office again. It had been made clear to him that he was covering Shields's caseload, but it wasn't yet clear whether this was a permanent assignment. Shields was on extended leave, but nothing official had been announced. Everyone knew about Mark's accident and assumed that was why he was not working. A few people knew his injuries weren't serious enough to justify an extended leave of absence, so the rumor mill was beginning to grind.

* * * * *

Mark Shields returned to the motel room he had been occupying for the past few days. His messages to Margaret at the house remained unanswered. Her cell phone had been disconnected, and her family didn't answer his calls or return his messages.

The next morning, he received a visitor accompanied by a private security officer. After being asked for his name, Shields confirmed that he was, in fact, Detective Mark Shields. The visitor simply handed Shields an envelope, and the two men left.

His first thought was that he was being terminated from the department. He was almost relieved to see it was divorce papers from Margaret's family attorney. *Good riddance*, he thought as he opened another bottle of scotch.

Chapter 30

Sarah had begun her second quilting class, more advanced than the first. In this one, she would be making an actual quilt—not a large one, just a throw for her couch. She loved being in the shop with all the beautiful fabrics, and as it turned out, she was very good on the machine. It had been many years since she had sewn anything. She was still using her old machine at home, but she loved working with the fancy new ones in the shop. "Perhaps a new machine is in order," she told herself. She was still considering converting the guest room into a sewing room.

For her focus fabric, Sarah had chosen a floral pattern, which she would use for the border of her throw. Her couch was a soft brown, and the border fabric she chose featured flowers in shades of peach and pale yellow with sage-green leaves and stems. There was a touch of brown here and there in the center of the flowers and the veins of the leaves. She chose a brown inner border to complement it.

The pattern the group had chosen was a log cabin. She learned that the middle block was traditionally red, but because of her color scheme, she decided to use the same brown for her centers. She then chose an assortment of tone-on-tone fabrics in the colors that were in her border—darker shades for one side of the block and much lighter shades for the other side. The center of the quilt would have a scrappy look but would coordinate with the border. She purchased additional border fabric for the back since it would be on her couch and, when she was curled up in it, both sides would show.

She was disappointed that Frank was not taking this class too, but she knew she would see him Friday night. She hoped Amanda would be able to get some useful information from him. Lacey and Dottie from the first class were both taking the log cabin class. Lacey was doing a beautiful job, but Dottie's flamboyance was getting in her way as she struggled to concentrate on what she was doing. Her fabric was scattered everywhere, and she had trouble sticking with one step, always wanting to move ahead whether or not she was ready. "But I want to see what it will look like finished. Let's go ahead and make one square and cut the rest later," she pleaded.

Ruth good-naturedly told her that she would be able to develop her own style once she learned the basics, but in the class, it was important for everyone to be doing the same step and progressing step by step. "What we're doing now is cutting out all our fabrics. Then we will begin making the squares. Just be patient, Dottie dear. It will be worth it." Dottie groaned and returned to her cutting board.

Lacey had all her colors carefully coordinated and in neat piles. She had completed cutting all of the strips for the log cabin square and was ready to cut her borders. Ruth suggested that, since she and Sarah were both finished with their strip cutting, perhaps they would like to take a coffee break until the others caught up. There were three other people in the class, but they were all beginners who hadn't taken the beginning class, so Ruth was giving them more time.

At the coffeepot, Lacey asked Sarah about the killing in Cunningham Village. "Have the police found out who did it yet?"

"No. The killer apparently didn't leave any clues at all," Sarah responded. "They can't find anyone with a motive, although they may be looking at this one man. But the whole investigation is very hush-hush. No one seems to be able to get any solid information from the police."

"Have they arrested that man?" Lacey asked.

"No. I've seen him around the community, and I really doubt that he had anything to do with it, anyway," Sarah shared.

"What about that Frank fellow from our first class? Remember, he said his friend knows who did it. Have the police looked into that?"

"They know about it." She didn't offer any other information and was glad that Lacey hadn't joined the Friday night group. She was afraid Lacey would bring it up if she saw Frank. Changing the subject, Sarah said, "I love the fabrics you chose. Your quilt is going to look like an heirloom."

Lacy had chosen calicos in muted colors for one side of the Log Cabin block and a mottled cream for all the strips on the light side. "I didn't see your border, though. What will you use for that?" Sarah asked.

"I spoke with Ruth about making extra log cabin squares and not having a border. I think it will make it look more traditional."

"You're right. What a great idea." They returned to the classroom after their short break and continued with their lesson.

After class, Sarah spoke with Ruth briefly to inquire whether it would be okay to bring Barney to the Friday night group. She explained that he was a rescue and hadn't been left alone much but that he was very well-behaved. Ruth said it would be fine and that the group would enjoy having him there.

Sarah had an ulterior motive, however. It had occurred to her that Barney was the perfect one to put Frank at ease the night Amanda was coming to the meeting.

When she got home, she asked Barney, "Well, young man. How would you like to be involved in an undercover operation?" Barney, of course, smiled and wagged his tail. Whatever she suggested was just fine with him, whether he understood it or not. Together they went out to the backyard and played fetch with his new tennis ball. He was ecstatic to be running and playing with his favorite person in the world.

When they came back into the house, Sarah noticed that Barney had dragged his fleece bed into her room, along with several of his toys. "So. Do I understand you to say that you want to move into my room?" she asked him. He wagged his tail and most of his body. He started to jump up on her, but she raised one finger and said, "No, Barney." He immediately froze. "Sit," she said, and he did. "Good boy," she praised. Sarah gave him a tasty treat from the jar. "We'll have to keep working on that one, Barney. I don't want you jumping up on people Friday night. Let's go to my room and find a good place for your bed and toy box."

* * * * *

The letter he was dreading arrived that day. It was addressed to Detective Mark Shields and sent to his home address, but his mail was being forwarded to a post office box. He swallowed the half glass of scotch that was left and opened the envelope with trepidation. He scanned the letter quickly, seeing that a meeting had been set up for the following Thursday with his lieutenant and the chief. "That doesn't sound so bad," he told himself, "I can handle that. Besides, I have Gabe on my team. All is well." The scotch was gone, and he had been alone too long. He needed to get out. "I'll head to Barney's and see how the old gang is getting along."

* * * * *

Gabriel came back to his office, his stomach in knots. "They really put me through the wringer today," he told Officer Holmes. Amanda didn't know the details of the Shields inquiry. In fact, she had never met the man. Rumor had it that he was a drunk, made numerous errors in judgment, and in general was a detriment to the department. She didn't know what they were asking of Gabriel, but whatever it was, it was causing him a great deal of stress. She knew they were friends as well as partners and that Gabe was very worried about Mark. Her heart went out to him. He was a good man who loved his job and his family. But she had the feeling Shields would use Gabe's loyalty to his own advantage.

After work that night, Amanda decided to stop by Barney's. Most of the guys went there during their off hours, and it would be an opportunity to get to know her fellow officers in more relaxed surroundings. As she entered, she immediately caught the eye of a handsome man sitting alone at a corner table. He was not in uniform, but he had the look of a cop. He smiled at her and nodded. *Do I know him?* she wondered. She had met so many people in her short time in Middletown that she could only assume she did, so she smiled back. He motioned for her to join him. She headed for the table, and as she approached he asked, "What's your drink?"

"I'll have a Molson," she responded as she sat down. "I'm ashamed to have to ask this, but do I know you? I've met so many people lately that they're all running together."

"Well, you're in uniform, so I would say you know *of* me. But as far as I know, we've never met. Where are you assigned?" he asked. His eyes appeared somewhat out of focus.

"I'm assigned temporarily to assist Detective Gabriel while his partner is on leave. And you?"

"Well," he slurred, "I'm that partner who's on leave."

"Detective Shields?" she said.

"You got it."

"I'm glad to meet you, detective." She wished she hadn't agreed to have a drink. She wondered how she could get out of this awkward situation. Nothing occurred to her right away, so she laid a five on the table so it was clear that she was buying her own drink. They talked a while, but his sentences didn't really track, and he didn't seem to be tuned into what she said.

After the first drink, she excused herself, repeated that she was glad to meet him, and quickly left the bar. "So that's the infamous Mark Shields," she said to herself once she got outside. As she was getting into her car, she saw him come out of the restaurant and look up and down the street. She hoped he wasn't looking for her, but just in case she pulled out immediately and headed home.

Chapter 31

Katie began the meeting by announcing, "We have a guest tonight." Ruth was returning bolts of fabric to the shelves but looked over to greet the guest. "This is Amanda Holmes," Katie continued. "Amanda is a relatively new quilter, and we all welcome her to our group." Turning to Amanda, she added, "I hope you brought some of your work to show us." Amanda had brought her first quilt, a single Irish chain. Sarah was able to see that it was made with nine patches and solid squares with the colors arranged to reveal a simple chain running diagonally through the quilt. She loved it and made a mental note to make that pattern sometime. Amanda pulled the second quilt out of her bag.

"This one is my most recent quilt," she said, "and it's not quite finished. I have the borders to put on, and I was hoping you folks could help me choose the fabrics. I know that I should have chosen my borders first, but I'm hoping to be able to find something that looks good with these blocks." It appeared to be a complex pattern, and Sarah couldn't dissect it. Others seemed to be able to immediately see the individual blocks. She hoped she would get that skilled someday.

Ruth, having finished putting bolts away, entered the classroom and said, "I want to introduce our second guest tonight. This is Barney. He is Sarah's new ..." not knowing what kind of dog he was, she turned to Sarah and asked, "What is he, Sarah?"

"Well, we just have to say he's a *dog*. No one seems to have any idea what kind of dog he is. But I can vouch for the fact that he is the sweetest dog I've ever met and definitely the smartest. He's only been with me for a couple of weeks, but he's moved right into my home and my heart. I brought him tonight so everyone could meet him."

The class took turns scratching his ears and petting him. Barney went from one to another, enjoying the attention. He stopped at Frank and never went any farther. Frank slipped out of his chair and sat on the floor with him. They became fast friends.

As soon as the meeting resumed, Frank returned to his seat, and Barney curled up at his feet. Frank looked at Sarah and smiled. So did Barney.

Others in the group began pulling out their quilts or hand work. Frank sat quietly and when it was his turn, he said, rather embarrassed, that he had only made one quilt, a small one for his grandmother's table, but that he wanted to make another one. Everyone encouraged him and even suggested that he make a quilt for his bed. "It would be just like what you made in class, Frank," Ruth said. "You just make it bigger." Frank seemed very excited about the idea. "You can come in here when you have time and use the machine in the classroom."

"My grandma has a sewing machine, and she said I can use it."

"Okay. In fact, would you like to make one like Amanda's Irish chain?" Ruth asked. "I can help you make a nine patch. You can go home and make a bunch of them and then bring them here some Friday night, and we'll all help you put it together." Frank was so keyed up he couldn't stay in his chair.

"I'm going to start looking at colors, okay?" he asked.

"Of course," Ruth responded with a big smile. She loved seeing a new quilter's excitement.

"May I come with you to look?" Amanda asked Frank.

"Sure," he responded. He headed for the front of the store and Amanda joined him. Barney followed right behind with his pink tongue hanging out. Sarah recognized Barney's look of happiness.

Addressing Frank once they got into the front of the shop, "I'm Amanda, and this is my first time here." She lowered her voice and added privately, "I'm a little nervous."

"Oh, you don't need to be. These are very nice people. Come on and I'll show you around. Oh," he added, "I'm Frank."

He took her around to the fabrics, and they talked about what colors would make a nice Irish chain. She went back to the classroom and got her quilt for him to examine more closely. Later, he also took her to the snack table and told her she could get something any time she wanted. She asked about his table runner and he said, "I'll bring it next time to show you. Are you coming next week?"

"I sure am," Amanda replied enthusiastically. This was going to take longer than she had hoped. If she could only see him once a week, it was going to be hard to develop a trusting relationship with him. "Do you think you could meet me here sometime before Friday and help me decide what quilt to make next?" she asked on a whim.

"Gosh," he said, lowering his head. "I don't know much about it."

"Yes, but you have a good eye for color. I'll pick a pattern, and you could help me pick out fabrics. I really would like that," she added.

Frank looked pleased that she seemed to respect his opinion, and they sat down at the snack table and talked. They divided a donut three ways and shared a piece with Barney. Frank told Amanda about his job and asked if she worked. She hated to lie to him but told him she worked in a bookstore, which had been her cover in a previous sting operation. She was even able to get him to talk about his grandmother and how sad she had been since his grandfather died.

"One more visit with Frank," Amanda told Gabriel the next day, "and I think I'll have him talking about the murder. He's very trusting and open. I feel bad about deceiving him."

"It's for the greater good, Amanda. We might catch a killer with his information. In the meantime, you aren't hurting him any. He probably needs to talk about it, but he's afraid to," Gabriel said.

Frank had given Amanda his cell phone number, and she called him on Tuesday to see if he could meet her after work. He said he could, and she suggested they meet at the café across the street from Stitches. She said she would like to buy him dinner in exchange for helping her. He said he had just gotten paid and would buy his own and that he was happy to be helping her. "You're my new friend," he added proudly. She felt another pang of guilt.

* * * * *

As Mark Shields walked back to his motel room, he mulled over his current situation. He had been at Barney's every night for the past week, and it was starting to get old. He definitely needed a diversion. He thought about the pretty girl who came into the bar a few nights before. *Amber? Anna?* He wondered. *No. Amanda.* He remembered it was an old-fashioned name like his grandmother's name. He would keep going to Barney's and hope to run into her again.

And where else was there to go anyway? he asked himself. He had chosen a motel near Barney's so he wouldn't have to use his car. He figured he would be charged if he was picked up drinking. *That's all I need with the department on my tail.*

I'll go to their meeting, he thought, *and I just might take my union rep.* He mulled the idea over. *But then that tells them that I think they've got something on me. Maybe I'll go alone. I'll look more confident that way. Yes. I'll go alone, look them in the eye, and dare them to come down on me.*

He knew the union rep would tell him he was not obligated to incriminate himself and that he should talk as little as possible. He figured that all the gripes were internal. He would probably have heard from Internal Affairs if there had been citizens' complaints. *This can't be very serious. I've had commendations. They know what I'm worth to them.* He swallowed the last drop in his flask as he arrived at the motel door.

It's probably the drinking. He entered his shabby motel room, splashed water on his face, and looked into the scratched mirror. He tried to focus. *They don't have any idea the pressure I'm under with that nagging woman and her interfering family. But that's almost over.* He would miss the money. As a couple, they had unlimited funds, but the funds flowed from her trust funds and were totally under the control of Margaret and her family. It was emasculating, he told himself, further justifying his drinking.

If it's about the drinking, I'll offer to get help. That should cut them off at the pass. I've seen it work with other guys. But then he remembered the white car. *If it's about missing that car ... well ... people make mistakes.* He opened a bottle of scotch and tore the wrapper off a fresh paper cup.

The letter said to report to the chief's office at 8:00 in the morning. It was 2:00 in the morning already. *Six hours,* he told himself looking down at his watch. *Plenty of time.* He dialed for a wake-up call and filled the cup again. *But I'll take it easy on this stuff tonight.* He was unaware that it was much too late to take it easy.

He walked into police headquarters at 11:30 the next morning.

Chapter 32

The phone was ringing when Sarah came in from the backyard. It was Martha. Sarah again congratulated herself for getting the new telephone and caller ID service. "Hi, Martha," she answered proudly.

"Hi, Mom. I haven't talked to you for weeks. How are you?"

"I'm doing just great," she responded cheerfully. "I think I told you about the quilt class I was taking, didn't I?"

"Yes, Mom, you did. How was it?" Martha asked without the enthusiasm Sarah would like to hear from her daughter.

"It was fantastic. I made a table runner in the first class and am working on a throw for my couch. I'm having a great time with it."

"I'm glad, Mom. I was calling to see if you'd like to have dinner with me this Saturday night. I've invited several of the women from work, and I thought it would be a nice evening for you. I could pick you up in the afternoon, and you could help me get ready."

"Oh, Martha, I'm so sorry, but I'm busy Saturday." Sarah was pleased that Martha would suggest this, and she regretted that she had to refuse. "A friend of mine and I have tickets for a play in the city on Saturday. But that would have been fun. I'm truly sorry I won't be able to come."

"A friend?" Martha asked curiously. "Who is this friend?"

"His name is Charles Parker. He's a retired policeman, and we've been spending time together lately. He's a very nice man. You'll like him."

"I *will* like him? How serious is this anyway?" Sarah knew that tone. Martha didn't approve already. "What do you know about this man? Are you sure you should be going into the city with him?"

"Martha, I've spent lots of time with him already. And what do I know about him? I know that he is a very special friend, and I enjoy his company," Sarah replied firmly. "That's enough for me, and if it's not enough for you, I'm sorry."

In the silence that followed, Sarah reflected on how often she and Martha had had these power struggles. When Martha was a child, they struggled daily. Martha never wanted to be told what to do. Once Martha went away to school and Sarah to work, they became more tolerant of each other; however, as Sarah aged, Martha attempted to reverse the roles and control her mother's life.

Martha finally spoke, "Okay, Mother. If that's what you want."

Sarah resisted getting into an argument with her and simply said, "Thank you for inviting me, Martha. I'm sure it would have been fun. I hope we can do it another time."

"Do you plan to introduce me and Jason to this man?"

"Of course," Sarah responded enthusiastically. "I would love for you to meet all of my friends here in the community. In fact, we're planning a community picnic in a couple of weeks. That would be a great chance for you to meet Charles and Sophie and some of the others."

"I'll have to get back to you," Martha responded in a flat tone. Sarah knew that was not what Martha had in mind. She was not asking to meet Sarah's friends. She was asking how serious her mother was about Charles. But since it was none of Martha's concern, Sarah chose to ignore the unspoken question. Besides, she had no idea how serious it might become.

"That's fine," Sarah responded. "I'll let you know when the date has been finalized. And if you want to come, I'd love to have you." After they hung up, Sarah was rather glad this whole issue had come up. It had been worrying her because she knew she needed to introduce Charles to Martha and Jason at some point but wasn't looking forward to it. She hadn't dated in all the years since Jonathan died. At first, she had no desire to get involved again, and later, as she fell into the routine of her new life, she just didn't think about it anymore. She had learned to be happy on her own. And even though she knew it made no sense, a piece of her was remaining loyal to Jonathan.

But meeting Charles changed all that. There seemed to be an instant bond between them. Of course, they shared a bit of history. They each had suffered the loss of a spouse, and they each had been alone for many years. But there was something more that she just couldn't define. She enjoyed every minute she spent with him, even though she had only known him a few weeks. They enjoyed the same things: quiet meals together, walking in the park, and now, making plans to go into the city on a *real date*. He had asked her while they were having coffee at the center's coffee shop the previous week. She had been a bit flustered, but he had politely ignored it.

After hanging up with Martha, Sarah turned to Barney and said, "Wanna go for a walk?" Barney jumped up from his spot in the corner of the kitchen, ran in big circles, and finally grabbed his leash from the hook and dropped it at her feet. "You're getting so good with your new tricks," she praised, and reached into his cookie jar. Barney made one more circle, which entangled them both in his leash. Sarah straightened it out, grabbed her jean jacket, and they headed into town. She wanted to make a quick stop at Stitches.

The shop was almost a mile from the Village, but there was a park in between that made it a very pleasant walk. Halfway through the park, they met Charles going the other way. "Hey gal," he greeted her with a broad grin. "Where are you two going in such a hurry?" He kissed her cheek and scratched Barney's ear.

"We're going to Stitches for some thread. At least that's our excuse. We're actually out here to enjoy this beautiful autumn day."

"Do you mind if I walk along?"

"Well, we would love to have you walk along, but isn't that exactly the direction you came from?"

"I was really just enjoying the day as well. I decided to treat myself to breakfast at the café and a nice walk in the park." They walked the rest of the way, hand in hand, with Barney leading the way. All three were smiling.

After leaving Stitches, Sarah and Charles crossed the street to the café. They had left Barney in the quilt shop with Ruth while they went for a cup of coffee. As they entered the café, the waitress smiled at Charles and exclaimed, "You're back."

"Yes. I realized I needed one more cup of coffee to reach my target heart rate," he kidded.

"Well, you were only gone a few minutes, so we'll make that a refill," she said as she led them to a table. "And you, ma'am?" Sarah ordered coffee as well and, glancing across the street, saw Barney in the window looking right back at her. She thought she could see his tail wagging.

The two friends chatted for awhile, and then Sarah broached the subject of Andy. "Things are just not progressing, Charles. I wonder if we'll ever know what happened to him. You never got a chance to meet him, but you would have liked him. Andy was a kind, down-to-earth guy. He was always finding ways to help people. Did I tell you that he dug my garden?"

"You miss him, don't you?"

"I do, Charles. It just doesn't seem right for him to be gone and without closure. We all need to know what happened. Andy deserves that, too."

Charles nodded sympathetically. "I know. Maybe Gabriel's assistant will come up with something after she talks to Frank. Did she come to the class Friday night?"

"Yes, she came and she really seemed to make headway with Frank. They spent most of the evening together. He was laughing and talking with her and playing with Barney."

"Barney? Barney was there?" he seemed surprised.

"Yes. That was my brainstorm," she bragged. "I realized Barney could put anyone at ease, and it sure worked."

"Great," Charles responded. "She just might make some headway. She's young, but I sensed that she'll become a good cop in time. She listens. Lots of cops don't know how to do that, or maybe just don't remember." Mark Shields crossed his mind. He wondered when things changed for Mark. He had talked to a buddy who was in Shields's old unit in Boston. He said Shields had been one of their best.

"Where did you go?" Sarah asked.

"Oh, I was just thinking about cops. The job takes a lot out of some people and makes others stronger. It's a strange job."

"You miss it?" she asked.

"Yeah," he said regretfully. "Yeah, I do. But that was another time," he added smiling. "And today is now." He reached across the table and touched her hand. This time she was sure she blushed.

"Okay, enough of this seriousness," she said. "I want to talk to you about a project I have in mind." She hesitated, but he raised an eyebrow and looked interested, so she continued. "I'm thinking about finding a kid who knows how to use a hammer and nails. I want shelves for my fabric in my guest room. In fact, I want to convert that room to a sewing room," she said enthusiastically. "I'm tired of seeing my kitchen table covered with fabric and rulers and cutting mats."

"We don't need a kid," he responded. "I can do that."

"No. I could never ask you to do the work, but I was hoping you could help me with the design."

"Okay, we'll talk about the design now, and later we'll talk about my doing it. But what a great excuse," he added with a devious smile, "to spend more time with you."

Ignoring his flirtation, she grabbed a napkin and said, "Okay, this is what I'm thinking. First I need to find some wire baskets to keep the fabric in. We can measure the baskets and make the shelves that wide." She sketched out some shelves about five feet long and drew a tall rectangle at one end of the shelves.

"What's that?" he asked.

"That's a cabinet. I have an oak cabinet that I'm storing in my daughter's basement. It would be great for all the small things that I don't want to keep out but need to get to easily, like my scissors, rotary cutters, rulers, and various sewing supplies. I'll also use it for my fabric."

"Okay," he said reaching for the drawing. "Now, how about this?" He extended one of the shelves outward at the opposite end and drew legs on it. "A sewing table for your machine at this end," he suggested.

"Ingenious," she declared excitedly. "Perfect. You do know what you're doing, don't you?" she teased.

"Let's go home and get one of our cars," he suggested. "We'll drive into town and take a look at wire baskets and get some measurements. Also, I need to take a look at the room, okay?"

Sarah was beside herself with excitement. She loved new projects, and she loved the idea of working on this with Charles. "I have a futon at Martha's house as well. I think I'll have someone pick that up for me and get rid of the bed in that room. That will give me more space."

"Good idea," Charles responded. "Paul, over at the Security Office, has a truck and does odd jobs for people in his off hours. Let's talk to him about picking the stuff up. He probably has a buddy who could help him. He might even know someone who might want the bed."

Sarah suddenly realized this would involve Martha, and she really wasn't ready. "Let's hold off on that part until we get all our plans made," Sarah suggested.

"Sure," he responded, wondering why her tone had changed slightly. He hoped he wasn't moving in on her plans too fast. He had a tendency to take over, and he knew that this independent, capable woman wouldn't like that. "We'll take it one step at a time. Where would you like to start?" he asked.

"Finding the wire baskets, just as you said," she responded excitedly. She was so excited that she almost forgot to pick up Barney at Stitches.

Chapter 33

The desk sergeant looked embarrassed about delivering the chief's message. "I'm sorry, detective. The chief said you're late and he won't be available again for a few hours. He said for you to wait."

"The hell I will," Shields responded loudly. He left the station and grabbed a cab back to his house. The key still didn't work, of course, but he got in through the basement window, which he had done before. He spent the next hour on the telephone and hung up with a contented smile on his face. He put two suitcases on the bed and quickly packed his clothes. He went into the computer room to make sure there was nothing he needed. He found his personal documents and stuck them in his briefcase; then he took the picture of his mother off the wall and added that. He returned to the bedroom and closed the suitcases. He placed all the bags by the front door and made one last trip through the house to make sure he wasn't missing anything.

He remembered the safe and went into her room. He opened it. "Empty, of course," he muttered. "That bitch."

The cab driver returned as prearranged and helped him with his bags. They went back to the police station and, again, asked to see the chief. The desk sergeant made a quick call and returned to say that the chief wouldn't be available until the end of the day.

"That's okay. This will only take a second." He ignored the sergeant's objections and walked into the chief's office unannounced, laid his resignation on the desk, and turned to leave.

"What's this?" the chief asked with annoyance.

"My resignation. I'm out of here." He turned and slammed the door behind him. He wouldn't need this man's recommendation because he already had his old job back. He was soon to be back in the city where he belonged.

Chief Harmon sat stunned, absorbing what had just happened. On the one hand, he was rid of a big problem. On the other, could he let this man loose on another department with no warning? After giving it some thought, he decided he wouldn't initiate the call. If they called him for a reference, he would be honest. It sounded, though, like Shields already had his ducks in a row. *Yes, I'll wait and see if they call me.* He reached for his to-do list and crossed off one item: resolve the Shields issue.

As the plane took off, Shields took one last look at the town as it grew smaller and even more insignificant. *Why did I ever come here?* he wondered. *How could I have thought her money would make up for all that was missing?* He thought about his drinking and how it had come close to ruining his career. He realized he would have to address that issue. He handed the flight attendant a hundred dollar bill and said, "Keep the scotch flowing, sweetie."

* * * * *

"We've been permanently assigned to the Burgess case," Gabriel told Amanda.

"How did that happen? What about Shields?"

"He's gone. Resigned. I have no idea why or how it happened. Maybe he was encouraged to do it, but we'll probably hear through the grapevine one of these days. In the meantime, you and I have to put our heads together and get this case closed. What happened when you met with Frank last night?"

"I might have something, but I'm not hopeful. It turns out that his friend may not be the most reliable source. The young man who told Frank he knew who did it is a guy Frank was in special education with back in his school days. Frank went on to the workshop and learned a trade. He's working at a grocery store now and is pretty high functioning. His friend was never able to leave the workshop. He sounds limited and is prone to exaggerations, according to Frank. I'm on my way over there now to talk with him, but as I said, I'm not hopeful."

"Do you want me to go with you?" Gabe offered.

"No. I think I do this kind of thing best when I'm alone. It's a matter of building trust, and I don't find that uniforms or men help much in that direction," she added dryly. Gabe grunted and returned to his paperwork.

"I've found two other cases in Shields's drawer," Gabe said as Amanda was preparing to leave. "It doesn't look like anything has been done on them. Not sure how they slipped through the cracks, but we're going to have to get moving. I imagine, when I bring these cases to the lieutenant's attention, he'll assign them to us."

Amanda moaned her response on her way out of the office.

Chapter 34

Sarah and Charles met Paul in front of the security office. "Looks like a good day for moving," Paul called to Charles as he was getting out of his truck. "They were calling for rain, and my truck isn't covered, but the sky is clear. No sign of rain yet. How far are we going?"

"My daughter lives on the other side of town," Sarah said, joining the conversation. "It's only about twenty minutes away. She lives on Palomino Drive just south of ..."

"I know the section." Paul interrupted. "My brother lives over there. What's her address?"

"521," Sarah responded.

"Great. I know exactly where that is. Corner house, right?"

"Yes. How did you know that?" Sarah asked.

"My brother lives right across the street. I'll call ahead and have him help us with the heavy stuff. Why don't you folks follow me."

Charles was sitting in the passenger seat of Sarah's car as they followed behind Paul's truck. "Are you sure your daughter is okay with meeting me this way?" he asked.

"Yes, Charles," Sarah responded. She knew he was nervous about meeting Martha. "She'll be fine with meeting you this way. When I called her, I explained what we were doing with the guest room, and once she got used to the idea, she agreed it was a good use of the room. She seemed glad that you're going to be helping with the construction instead of some stranger." Sarah spoke confidently and reassuringly, but she was, in fact, more nervous than Charles about introducing them. She could never tell what Martha's mood would be, and Martha was quick to speak her mind with little concern for how her words might affect others.

They pulled up behind the truck right in front of Martha's house. "You sure did know exactly where you were going," Martha called to Paul.

"Yep. Here comes my brother now."

Paul was making the introductions as the front door opened. Martha came out, nodded at her mother, and turned to Paul's brother. "Are you going to be helping?" she asked coolly.

Sarah realized this must be the neighbor Martha had been complaining about. She had told her mother that there was a neighbor with teenage kids that she described as having "no consideration for others." Upon questioning Martha, her only complaint seemed to be loud music. Sarah was sometimes glad that Martha had not had children. "She just doesn't have the temperament for it," she had said to Sophie.

As Paul and his brother talked, Sarah pulled Charles aside and said, "Martha, I want you to meet my good friend, Charles Parker. Charles, this is my daughter, Martha."

Martha extended her hand, looked him in the eye, and said, "I'm glad to meet you, Mr. Parker."

"Call me Charles," he said with a smile. "I'm glad to meet you, too. Your mother has told me so much about you. She's very proud of you." Martha seemed surprised and looked at her mother questioningly. Not wanting to get into anything with Martha, she simply smiled and suggested they show the men what they were picking up.

"Come on, fellas," Sarah called out.

"Okay," Paul said, following Sarah toward the house. "What're we getting?"

"There's a futon and a wooden cabinet in the basement." Paul frowned. "In the basement, huh?"

Martha spoke up and told them there was an outside door on the side of the house that went directly into the basement.

"No steps involved," Sarah reassured them. Paul and his brother had the truck loaded in a matter of minutes and were ready to leave. Martha asked if anyone wanted a cup of coffee before they left. Paul said he would like to have a few minutes to run across the street and say hello to his brother's family, and Sarah said she and Charles would love to stay for a few minutes. "Take your time," Sarah called to Paul as he and his brother headed across the street.

When they walked into the kitchen, Sarah was surprised to find the table already set for coffee. The room was filled with the aroma of freshly brewed coffee, and Martha pulled a coffee cake from the oven, which was set on warm. Sarah was very glad they had accepted her invitation. Martha had clearly planned for them to stay.

As they drank coffee, Martha asked about the plans for the sewing room. Charles pulled a small notebook out of his breast pocket and began to sketch the plans. Sarah momentarily pictured him as a young officer, reaching for his notebook. She wondered what he was like when he first entered the police force. "Are you still with us?" Charles asked, smiling.

"Oh, sorry. Yes, I'm right here. What do you think of the plans, Martha?"

"I think it looks great, Mother. I don't know anything about sewing and what you might need, but this looks like you've thought of everything." Martha and Charles continued to talk about the plans. Martha asked her mother what tools she used. After Sarah described the measuring and cutting tools, Martha suggested a pegboard above the worktable, and both Sarah and Charles loved the idea.

"Why don't you come over next week," Sarah asked. "We could have lunch and walk over to the fabric shop. I'd love to show you what I'm working on and introduce you to my teachers."

"I'd like that," Martha said simply.

On the way home, Sarah thought about Martha. She saw her soften, and she hadn't seen that side of Martha for many years. She wondered if seeing her with Charles had anything to do with it. She wished Martha had someone in her life that she could relax around and begin to enjoy life again. She had been so hurt by the loss of her father, and later her own divorce, that she seemed to have just hardened. Today she revealed a crack in that shell.

Chapter 35

It was late afternoon, and Detective Amanda Holmes was rushing to the workshop before it closed for the day when her cell phone rang. It was Gabe. "But I'm on my way to the workshop to meet with Frank's friend." Amanda objected. "Do you really need me right now, Gabe?" Amanda swerved to miss the car that had cut in front of her to make an illegal turn. If she weren't in such a hurry, she would have pulled him over, but instead she just turned on the siren to give him a scare.

"Yes, we need to get over there right away," Detective Gabriel responded. "There was a disturbance call from Cunningham Village, and the lieutenant wants us out there. That's all I know except that it's at the home of Ralph and Millie Lake."

"Am I supposed to know them?" Amanda asked.

"Yes ... from the Burgess file. Millie is the one who was reported to have had an affair with Andrew Burgess. Ralph is her husband and the guy we interviewed a couple of weeks ago. You weren't involved yet."

"Ah, yes. The angry drunk."

"That's the guy," Gabe responded. *At least that's one of the angry drunks involved in that interview*, he thought.

When they arrived at the Lake's house, they found Ralph on the front porch in handcuffs, and Millie wrapped around him sobbing. "What's going on here?" Detective Gabriel asked, addressing the officer who appeared to be in charge.

"We had a call from a neighbor about a disturbance at this address. We found Mrs. Lake on the floor and this guy standing over her, yelling. We cuffed him, and now she's pleading with us to let him go. She swears they were just having a disagreement and that he didn't hit her. Her face is already swollen and red."

Gabe turned to her. She attempted to stop sobbing and said, "I fell. That's all. I just fell."

Gabe turned to Ralph. "We meet again, Mr. Lake. What's going on here?"

"It's like she said. The bitch fell. I was just helping her up," he slurred.

"Let's take this down to the station." Gabe turned to Amanda and added, "You take Mrs. Lake." Then, addressing one of the officers, he added, "Read him his rights, and I'll meet you there."

Detective Gabriel got into his car and drove off. Amanda helped Millie Lake into her patrol car but didn't drive away immediately. Instead, she turned to Millie and asked, "Are you okay? Do you need to go by the hospital and get checked out?"

"No." She said emphatically. "Ralph would kill me."

"Kill you?" Amanda asked with raised eyebrows.

"No … not actually *kill* me … but he would be furious. I don't want to make him any angrier than he already is.

Once he sobers up, he'll be fine." Millie paused, and then added, "They aren't going to put him in jail are they?"

Amanda didn't answer her question, and the two women drove to the police station in silence. Once they arrived, Amanda took Millie to a small interrogation room on the main corridor. It was a less intimating room and was often used for questioning witnesses and families of the accused. She offered Millie coffee but told her it was actually not very good. "How about a soda?" she suggested instead. Millie nodded. Amanda left the room and returned with two sodas and a couple of packages of vending machine cookies.

"Tell me what happened, Millie. What made him so angry?" Amanda spoke softly.

Millie started to say she had fallen, but Amanda cut her off, "No, Millie. I know better. Please … just talk to me." Millie began to cry softly. Amanda waited without speaking. Finally Millie spoke.

"Ralph loves me. I want you to know that first off. But he has this problem with his temper. Actually, it's only when he's drinking, but that's pretty often. And he just … sort of … loses control sometimes."

"He hits you?" Amanda asked. Millie remained quiet. "Did he hit you tonight?" Millie began to sob.

"Yes," she said finally. "I didn't think he was going to stop this time," she added softly.

"What set him off?" Amanda asked.

"He was laid off from his job today, and he wasn't expecting it. The factory had lost a couple of contracts, and other guys were thinking they might get laid off, but Ralph said they needed him, whether they had the contracts or not. He was just blindsided by it. He didn't even come home … he went directly to the bar and came home cussing and yelling. I asked what had happened, and that's when he turned on me." She began to sob again and cover her eyes with embarrassment.

Trying to catch her totally off guard, Amanda asked abruptly, "Do you think he killed Andy?"

Amanda had surprised Millie with the question, and Millie raised her head, responding adamantly, "No. Absolutely not. Ralph could never do that. He can be mean, but he's no killer."

"The detectives are going to want to talk to you, Millie. Please tell them the truth. I know you think things will work out, but you could have been killed tonight. I want you to take that seriously." Amanda watched as Millie slightly nodded her head as if she hesitantly agreed.

"If you ever want to get out of this situation or need help," Amanda added, "let me know. I'll help in any way I can." She wrote her private number on the back of her card and handed it to Millie. She also handed her a card for the local women's shelter. "These folks can help you, too."

Millie lowered her head and said quietly, "Thank you." She hesitated and then added, "I don't know who I've become." Amanda waited at first, but Millie didn't say anything else. Amanda then stood and said, "I'll let the detectives know you're here."

To Amanda's surprise, Millie agreed to file charges later that night. By the time Amanda got home, it was almost dawn. She collapsed into bed and immediately fell asleep.

* * * * *

Since Lake was arrested for assault, they now had his fingerprints. Detective Gabriel requested that the lab compare them to the unidentified sets found in the Burgess house. As it turned out, there were several matches in the living room and on the front door frame. Gabe thought about where they were with the case. *We have a possible motive: the affair. Now we have prints.* Lake had an alibi, but the department was unable to confirm it. The bartender knew him but wasn't sure if he was at Barney's that particular night. The friends who tentatively said he was there could have been covering for him. *This just might be our guy,* he told himself hopefully. He met with his lieutenant and the prosecutor early the next morning, and they decided to file murder charges.

Millie Lake appeared at the station early the next morning with a lawyer and managed to have the charges against him dropped for the assault on her. She was prepared to take him home but learned that he had now been arrested for murder. Millie became hysterical, sobbing that he was innocent. She asked to see Detective Holmes, but she was not available. She also asked to see her husband, but she was told she would have to wait.

Detective Amanda Holmes was called and arrived at the courthouse just in time for Ralph Lake's hearing.

Chapter 36

Sarah and Charles had carried the shelves and brackets into the guest room. "I think we're ready to start," Charles announced. The bed was gone, and the new items were stacked against one wall. While Charles was measuring, Sarah stood quietly staring out of the window. "What's wrong, lady?" he asked.

"I was thinking about Andy's case. Ralph Lake has been arrested for his murder, and that just doesn't sit right with me. Something's wrong. I tried to call Millie, but there was no answer."

Sarah told Charles she needed to talk to Sophie, and he assured her he would be fine working on his own for a while. He would install all the brackets and then would need her to help him place the shelves. He had built the sewing table extension at his house and brought it when he came. She gave him a light kiss on the cheek and left.

"I'm sorry I didn't call first, Sophie. May I come in?"

"Of course, kiddo. Come on in," Sophie replied. "I wanted to talk to you anyway, but I saw your pretty boy's car in front of your house early this morning and didn't want to disturb anything." She waggled her eyebrows Groucho Marx style.

"Be serious, Sophie," Sarah said, defending herself. "He's just there to help with the shelves."

"Um hmm."

"I want to talk about this Lake thing," Sarah said as they walked into the kitchen.

Assuming a more serious tone, Sophie said, "I wanted to talk to you about that, too. I've tried to call Millie this morning, but there's no answer." Sophie and Millie had been friends since they moved into the Village years before. She and Millie used to do many of the activities together, but in the past few years, Millie didn't go out much. "Problems at home," Sophie had explained.

"So I called Alice, who lives next door to the Lakes," Sophie continued as she started the coffee. "She said Millie went off with the police last night and came home in a squad car early this morning. She said she was home for a few hours and drove off around 9:00 this morning."

Sarah thought about that, shaking her head and frowning. "I just don't know. Something doesn't feel right. I want to talk to Millie. Where do you suppose she is?"

"Let's call Detective Gabriel," Sophie suggested. They immediately dialed the number and were told the detective was not available. As they were starting to leave a message, the sergeant put Officer Holmes on the line.

"Hello, this is Amanda Holmes."

"Good morning, officer. This is Sarah Miller, and Sophie Ward is here with me. We wanted to ask you a couple of questions about the Lakes."

"Yes?" Her friendly tone turned guarded.

"We've been trying to reach Millie Lake, but there's no answer. We were wondering if she's okay and thought perhaps you or Detective Gabriel would know something about it."

"Well, I assume they're on their way home," she responded.

"They?"

"Yes," she responded in an exasperated tone. "They," she emphasized. "Mrs. Lake bailed her husband out just a few minutes ago. They're probably home by now."

"How could that happen? I thought he was arrested for murder."

"Well, according to the prosecutor, our evidence was weak. The judge set bail low, and Mrs. Lake jumped right in and bailed him out," Amanda added with growing irritation in her voice.

After they got off the phone, Sarah told Sophie about the conversation, and they sat without talking for a while. "I don't get it," Sophie finally said. "People get out on bail, so he will still be tried. Why do you suppose Officer Amanda is so upset?"

* * * * *

Amanda Holmes sat at her desk staring out the streaked station house window. She had only been in the department a couple of months and already she had seen several women choose life with their abusers over their own safety. She was surprised to see Millie Lake at her husband's hearing and noticed that Millie dropped her eyes when Amanda looked her way.

Amanda Holmes was a strong, independent woman and couldn't understand why anyone would choose to live in a dangerous situation. She would hear the women making excuses for their men: "He didn't mean it." "It was my fault." "He always apologizes the next day...." "I know he loves me."

"Don't women know they have choices?" she muttered to herself impatiently. She shook her head but knew she would not stop trying to make a difference. She had watched her mother live under the total control of a cruel drunk. Amanda got away the day she graduated from high school. Her mother chose to stay, despite Amanda's efforts to help her.

Amanda sighed and picked up one of the files Detective Shields had left untouched.

* * * * *

When Sarah got back home, she was shocked to see how much Charles had accomplished. He not only had the braces installed, but had the bottom shelf in place as well as the extension for her sewing machine. "Let's see how your machine looks on here," he said as she admired his handiwork. Sarah rolled the machine out of the closet and unzipped the case. Charles pulled it out and put it on the table. It exactly fit and made a perfect sewing station.

Above the sewing table, he was in the process of installing a piece of pegboard. He had purchased hooks of different shapes and sizes so she could hang all her tools. Along the bottom, he was inserting a row of very thin pegs. "What are those for?" Sarah asked, looking at the little pegs.

"Those are for your thread," he answered with a smile.

"How do you know all this?" Sarah asked in amazement.

She saw a look of sadness cross his face momentarily, but then he simply smiled and shrugged. *Such a nice man. Gentle, kind, and thoughtful.* She knew his wife had been sick for several years before she died, and Sarah knew he would have given her excellent care. He didn't talk about his wife often. It had happened only once, actually, and that was when they were getting to know each other. It was clearly a painful thing for him to even think about.

"Martha will be overjoyed when she sees that we used her idea," Sarah said, changing the subject. "She loves to make suggestions, and I so rarely take her up on them. I must admit that this was a great idea." Sarah had probably not resisted Martha's suggestion this time because Charles was right there. Otherwise, she probably would have objected, just like she fought against the answering machine and even moving to Cunningham Village. She told herself that she would try to be more open to Martha in the future. These were, in fact, three good ideas.

After they completed the project and moved all the furniture back into the room, Sarah stood back and looked at her new sewing room. She had placed her supplies on the pegboard, along with what few spools of thread she had, and she lovingly placed her few pieces of fabric neatly on shelves in the oak cabinet. "It needs more stash," she said defiantly and vowed to go shopping the very next day.

That evening she poured herself a cup of herbal tea and sat down in the living room. She had intended to watch television, but her mind kept wandering to Andy's murder. She just didn't feel comfortable with the route the police were taking. She had only known Millie and Ralph for a few months, but Sophie had known them for years. Andy had been a close friend of Ralph's throughout those years. Sophie said they had always been close and that Millie and Andy seemed to have a close friendship, but she had never had any feeling there was "hanky-panky," as Sophie put it. "Andy was just her friend," Sophie had said.

Sarah called Sophie despite the hour. She knew Sophie was still up because she could see the flickering light from her television through the curtains. "Hello, kiddo," she answered. "Are you thinking about the same thing I am?"

"I think so," Sarah responded. "I really want to talk to Millie."

"Me, too. Let's invite her to lunch tomorrow. I'll fix something here."

"I think she might feel less intimidated if we invite her out somewhere," Sarah suggested. "I was thinking maybe we could just go to the café. What do you think?"

Sophie agreed and said she would call Millie since she knew her best. "We go out to lunch every couple of months anyway," Sophie said. They decided to try to set it up for the next day.

When Sophie called Sarah back the next morning, she said that Millie seemed eager to get together. Sophie didn't mention that Sarah would be there for fear of scaring her off.

Chapter 37

It was a beautiful autumn day, and Sarah decided to walk through the park and stop by Stitches before she met Sophie and Millie at the café. She wished she could bring Barney with her, but she wasn't sure how long she'd be at the café, and she didn't want to leave Barney at the fabric shop too long.

She saw Sophie's car pull up at 12:30, and the two women enter the café. She paid for her fabric and strolled over casually. As she walked in, Sophie called out in her usual boisterous voice, "Hey kiddo, come sit with us." Millie looked surprised but smiled at Sarah. Obviously, Sophie had not told Millie that Sarah would be joining them.

Sarah joined the women, and they all ordered. The conversation was light, and Millie laughed several times at Sophie's raucous stories. After they finished dessert and were sipping their coffee, Sarah turned to Millie and said, "I'm so sorry about Ralph, Millie. I know that must be terrible for you. Why in the world would the police think such an outrageous thing? We all know Ralph couldn't have killed Andy."

Millie was clearly taken aback by the directness of Sarah's question, but after a moment's hesitation she responded.

"I'm sure you've both heard tales about me and Ralph, and some of those stories are true. He can get mean when he's drinking. He hit me a time or two, and everyone knows about that."

Sarah started to shake her head, but Millie stopped her. "I know what people are saying, Sarah. What they don't know is that he loves me and he always apologizes. There are reasons for the way he gets, and I try to be understanding." Again, she paused, and then she added, looking Sarah right in the eye, "Yes, Ralph has a temper and he can be mean, but Ralph is *not* a killer." She hesitated as if deciding whether to go on.

"Go on, Millie. Please," Sarah said gently. "We care about you, and we want to understand what's happened."

"I want the two of you to know the whole story," Millie began. "There are already too many rumors flying around. "This all started a couple of months ago. Ralph heard those cruel rumors about me and Andy, and he just about went crazy." Again, Sarah started to deny hearing about it, but Millie interrupted her saying, "Sarah, Sophie told me you both heard the rumors, and I want you both to know they aren't true." She looked at Sarah with tears in her eyes, and added, "Please believe me."

After a few moments, Millie continued, "I tried to tell Ralph there was nothing to it. Andy and I were just good friends. Andy was good friends with both of us, but Ralph wouldn't listen. He kept bringing it up, and each time he would get angrier and more violent. This one night when he came home, he had been drinking—maybe not as much as other times, but some. He seemed to be angrier with Andy this time than with me. Suddenly he slammed out of the house and drove off in his car. He didn't come back that night."

"Was that the night Andy was killed?" Sarah asked with trepidation.

"No. This happened a week or so before that," Millie responded. "Anyway," she continued, "Ralph came home the next morning. He told me he was sorry, kissed me goodbye, and left for work. He didn't tell me where he had been, and I didn't ask."

"Did you ever find out where he had been?" Sophie asked.

"Yes. Andy called me later that day," Millie responded, "and told me that Ralph had banged on his door the night before and was fuming mad. But somehow Andy was able to get him settled down. Andy was good at that. He seemed to understand Ralph better than anyone. Andy was able to convince Ralph that the rumors were just that—rumors." Millie took a sip of her coffee, and Sarah noticed her hands were shaking. Sarah took her hand gently in her own.

Sophie spoke more quietly than usual and said, "Tell us what happened then. Did they make up?"

"Ralph and Andy had been friends for years," Millie continued. "Good friends. Andy was somehow able to get Ralph to relax. Andy didn't drink anymore, but he had a bottle in the house, and he gave Ralph a couple of drinks. They ended up talking for hours. Andy told me he learned some things about Ralph he never knew. He said, 'There's a good guy in there under all that rage.' Ralph ended up sleeping on Andy's couch that night."

"Would you like another cup of coffee, Millie? I'm sure that's cold," Sarah asked, noticing that Millie was again sipping her coffee.

"I think I would like tea. Do they have decaffeinated here?" Millie asked. Sophie signaled for the waitress, and Sarah ordered herbal tea for everyone. Millie thanked her and excused herself to go to the ladies room. Sophie expressed concern that she might not come back, but Millie returned right away and looked somewhat refreshed. "I splashed water on my face," she explained with a weak smile as she sat down.

After the waitress served the tea, Sophie said, "Okay, where were we?"

"I think we left poor Ralph tossing and turning on Andy's lumpy couch," Sophie offered in an attempt to lighten the mood somewhat.

"Yes. Andy told me that the next morning they had coffee, shook hands, and Ralph left to come home."

The women were quiet for a while as Sophie and Sarah let this barrage of information settle in. Suddenly Millie sat tall, squared her shoulders, and spoke with determination, "I know Ralph didn't kill Andy," she said. "I know that. Andy was killed just a few days after Ralph was with him. They talked on the phone the day before Andy was killed. I heard Ralph laughing with Andy. They had worked out their differences. Why would Ralph kill him?"

"Was Ralph home the night Andy was killed?" Sarah asked cautiously, not wanting to alienate her new friend.

"He went out that night for a while, but he came home early and was in a good mood. We were closer that night than we've been for a very long time," she added with a trace of a blush on her cheeks.

"Did you tell the police all this when he was arrested?" Sarah asked.

"Yes, but they didn't believe me," she said. "This gets complicated, but I need to explain this part. You know he was arrested for something else two nights ago, right?" Both women shook their heads and looked surprised.

"For what," Sophie asked in disbelief.

"Well, unfortunately, the police were called that night because of the noise. Ralph had way too much to drink because he was laid off that day. He went straight to the bar and came home in the middle of the night in a rage."

Millie dropped her eyes and looked embarrassed. "He hit me that night and yelled obscenities. He was very drunk, and our next door neighbor called the police. It was the first time he had lost his temper since that night about Andy. The police took him away, and this woman officer talked me into filing charges. I was immediately sorry, and the next morning I went to get him out. In the meantime, they had somehow connected him to Andy's death. I guess you know he's been charged," she added, beginning to sob. "But he didn't do it. I know that in my heart."

"Is he back home now?" Sophie asked, knowing the answer already.

"Yes, he's home temporarily," Millie said, wiping her eyes. "I need to find a lawyer. They assigned him a public defender, but I don't know if he'll be any good."

Sophie and Sarah looked at each other but didn't know what to say. Finally Sarah spoke. "Millie, you know we care about you. We want to help but don't know how. What can we do?"

"It means more than you can imagine that you would even want to get involved in this mess." Tears ran down

Millie's cheeks, and her face sagged with exhaustion. "Just letting me talk is help enough," she added.

"I think right now the best thing would be for you go home and get some rest," Sarah offered. "Would you like for us to check around about the attorney? I have a friend who worked in the criminal justice system before he retired. He would probably know the attorney you were assigned, and if necessary, he could give you a better referral."

"I would appreciate that, Sarah. You've been so kind."

"Sophie and I care about you, and Andy was a dear friend of ours. We can both understand how you became close to him. He was a kind and understanding man."

"That's exactly it," Millie said with a hint of enthusiasm. "He listened to me. I could talk to him about my relationship with Ralph, and he never judged me or Ralph. He was the most understanding man I've ever known. He truly cared about both of us."

"Let's get together again, Millie," Sarah was saying as they got their things together and prepared to leave. "But in the meantime, I want you to call me if you need to talk or just want to get out of the house for a while." Millie thanked her with tears in her eyes, and the two women hugged. Sophie stepped back almost imperceptibly, but enough for Sarah to notice. *Sophie is not a hugger*, she realized.

When she got home, Sarah felt exhausted. It had been an emotional afternoon, and she was drained. She hoped Sophie wouldn't want to dissect what they'd learned today. She just wanted to curl up on the couch with Barney and let it all sink in. And that's exactly what she did.

Chapter 38

Barney jumped on the bed and began licking Sarah's face. "Barney. Get down. You know better," Sarah shouted. Barney slithered off the bed and hid his head under her dust ruffle. Sarah immediately felt terrible for yelling at him. "I was asleep and you surprised me, little fellow." She bent over and patted his neck at the point where it disappeared under the bed. "I'm sorry, sweet dog. I'll never yell at you again. I know I scared you." Barney twisted sideways so his head came part of the way out from under the bed. With his chin flat on the floor, he rolled his eyes upward and looked at her with a most pathetic and forlorn look.

"I know you would like me to think you're totally destroyed by my actions, my dear dog. But unfortunately for you, your tail is starting to wag ... and as you know, that's a dead giveaway." Barney scampered to his feet and snuggled his neck against hers, taking advantage of the fact that she was bending down and closer to his height. They hugged for a while before she interrupted the lovefest and said, "How about some breakfast?" All was forgiven. Barney ran in his happy circles, and they headed for the kitchen.

Sarah opened the back door for him and left it open a crack so he could get back in. Moments later he was back and wagging his whole body as she opened his can of dog food. She put just a few spoons full into his bowl of kibbles, and he attacked it like he hadn't had a bite for weeks. He followed his breakfast with enthusiastic slurps from his water bowl, splashing water all over his corner of the kitchen. She handed him a dessert treat and gave him an ear scratch. "What did I ever do without you," she asked as she sopped up the water. He smiled.

Sarah ate her own breakfast and decided to talk with Sophie about yesterday's visit with Millie. She had come to several conclusions and wanted Sophie's thoughts. For one thing, she wasn't sure they could completely trust Millie's version of Ralph's encounter with Andy. It seemed a bit convenient in that it took away something the police thought they had—a motive. And she said Ralph came home early the night Andy was killed, which took the second thing away—opportunity. Without motive and opportunity, the prosecutor would have difficulty making his case. Ralph had been to Andy's house, so perhaps there were fingerprints, but since they were friends, that could have happened at any time.

Sarah called Sophie. When Sophie answered, Sarah didn't even identify herself but simply said, "Did he do it, or not?"

"I see you're thinking along the same lines I am. I have no idea. But I know she loves him enough to lie for him."

"But maybe he's innocent," Sarah said.

"Maybe he is."

"Maybe she did it," Sarah added reluctantly.

"Maybe she did."

They remained quiet for awhile, and then Sophie said, "Come on over here, girl. This needs collaboration."

Sarah snapped the leash on Barney and took him with her. "Why did you bring that ugly beast?" Sophie asked, attempting to look annoyed.

"I brought him because I know you love him and he misses his Aunty Sophie."

"Humph."

They sat down to their usual coffee and cookies, but neither had much to say. Barney laid his head on Sophie's lap, and she casually scratched his ear. He curled up by her feet, rested his head on his outstretched paws, and closed his eyes. Finally Sarah spoke. "I don't know what to think. But if Ralph is innocent, then someone else is guilty."

"Brilliant deduction, inspector," Sophie said in as serious a voice as she could muster.

"Okay, Sophie. I know that may sound silly, but it tells us what we need to do. We need to find the person who did it. The police are finished because they have Ralph. They won't be looking anymore."

"And you think we can do that?" Sophie asked.

"I think we need to do it if there's any possibility Millie is telling the truth and Ralph is innocent."

"Where would we start?" Sophie asked, hoping Sarah had an idea because she sure had none.

"Let's start with a list of who we think could have done it. First of all, I think Frank's friend knows something, and we should talk to him. Amanda Holmes was going to do that, but I'm sure she won't be pursuing that clue now since they think they have their man, right?"

"I think you're probably right," Sophie responded. Then she added, "No one ever talks about that scruffy looking man who came to the funeral. Who was that guy anyway? No one seemed to know him. Maybe *he* did it."

"We could send out the word again and see if anyone knows who he was," Sarah suggested. "And there's always the possibility of a random robbery gone bad, even though security says there's no way anyone could get past them. The white car got past them."

"Yes," Sophie shouted. "The white car. I had forgotten about that. Didn't we originally think the killer was driving the white car? Whatever happened to that theory?"

"Detective Shields was supposedly following up on that. By the way, what do you suppose happened to Shields?"

"Don't ask," Sophie groaned. "It was good riddance as far as I'm concerned,"

The two women went over all the possibilities and decided to start with Frank's friend. "I'll need to get back to Frank to get the guy's name. Amanda knows, but I don't want to alert the police that we're looking around."

"I agree," Sophie said. "You talk to Frank, and we'll go see his friend together. In the meantime, I'm going to call a few of my contacts and put some feelers out about the 'scruffy guy,' as you call him. I just had a thought … maybe he left in the white car."

"Well, that's speculation that can't be proven. Let's try to stick with what we can confirm."

"Always the logical one." Sophie sputtered. "Let's get on it, kiddo."

* * * * *

Sarah had been careful not to upset Frank by asking about his friend, but now she had to toss care to the wind and just ask him. Perhaps she could explain why she wanted to know and he would understand. It was Friday morning, and she could only hope Frank would be at the quilt meeting that night. He didn't always come, but Ruth had him excited about a quilt idea, so there was a pretty good chance he would be there.

She spent the afternoon in her new sewing room, rearranging the few things she had and sewing a few seams on her throw for class. She was beginning to see what it was going to look like finished, and she felt it would be perfect in her living room. She hoped no one would notice the small errors she had made along the way. *Perhaps those can be my "humility blocks,"* she thought. According to folklore, Ruth had explained, Amish quilters sometimes included an intentional error as a tribute to God and the fact that only He could produce perfection.

Chapter 39

Sarah had an early supper and decided to take Barney for a long walk in the park before the quilt club meeting. Barney had been especially excited about the leaves. This was his first autumn living in a home where he didn't have to worry about searching for his next meal. He had time to play, and the softly blowing leaves were perfect toys. He bounced on them like a cat and ran through piled leaves, scattering them every which way. Sarah looked around, hoping no one was watching. She was feeling guilty about all the time her neighbors had spent neatly piling the leaves. *But Barney is smiling, and isn't that more important than neatly piled leaves?* she asked herself.

They spent so much time in the park that Sarah decided she should just go directly to her meeting at Stitches. Everyone seemed to enjoy having Barney there, and after he greeted each person individually, he usually curled up and went to sleep. They got there early, and Frank was already looking at fabric. Sarah was delighted. She told him right away that she needed to talk with him, and they went into the small break room and she got them sodas.

Sarah began by telling Frank that she was glad he had talked to Amanda and helped her plan her quilt. Frank scratched Barney's ears while they sat and talked and seemed very comfortable.

Sarah decided to go right into talking about Andy's death and her desire to help find the person who did it. "He was a very good friend of mine and someone I really cared about. I want to find out what happened to him, but I think the police are on the wrong track." Frank stopped scratching Barney and gave Sarah his full attention. "I know you don't want to talk about this, Frank, but I think you can help me."

"Me?"

"Yes, Frank. Remember when you told me that your friend knows who did it?"

"Yes." He said softly, looking down. "But he doesn't know exactly who it was."

"What do you mean, Frank?"

"This is a secret, but I guess I can tell you since you're trying to help. My friend's name is Billie, and he's still back in the workshop. He can't work because he just doesn't understand stuff. Maybe he'll be able to help me at the grocery store someday. He told me he's learning how."

"That will be good, Frank. I'm sure you would be happy to have him working with you, but can we get back to my friend. His name was Andy, and he was a very kind man. Can you tell me what your friend knows about his death?"

"He doesn't really know who did it. He saw someone leaving the house where the man was killed."

"He did?" Sarah asked with excitement. "Who did he see?"

"He doesn't know her name. He just saw her leave."

"*Her?* It was a woman?" Sarah was astounded. "He saw a woman leave Andy's house?" She wondered who it could have been, and even if this was reliable information.

"Does Billie live near Andy's house?"

"Right across the street. He lives with his grandma, too." Sarah wondered if she should talk directly to Billie, but Frank seemed very clear. Sarah was so stunned by what Frank had told her that she didn't think she could even stay for the meeting. She felt a strong need to talk to Sophie right away. When Ruth came in, Sarah spoke with her briefly, making an excuse for not staying. She said goodbye to Frank and, in a whisper, thanked him for helping her. She told him she would see him the next week.

Outside the shop, Sarah called Charles and asked him if he could come pick her up. She said she had some very interesting information. Of course, he agreed to come right away. He would never miss an opportunity to spend time with this lovely woman he was growing very close to. It felt incredibly good to have someone to care about again. He hadn't thought this could happen. He hadn't shared his feelings with Sarah because he didn't want to scare her off. *Someday*, he told himself. *Someday.*

Sarah started walking slowly up the street, and within minutes, she spotted Charles's car. Just as the car stopped, Sarah and Barney jumped in, Sarah in the front and Barney, of course, stretching out on the back seat after giving Charles a sloppy lick on his ear. "And you?" Charles said, turning to Sarah.

"Well, I can give you a little kiss, but I won't lick your ear." They both laughed, and Sarah moved closer to him.

She felt warm against him, and he took her hand as he drove off.

"Okay, lady. What's going on?" he asked.

"Frank told me his friend saw a woman leave Andy's house the night he was killed," Sarah announced incredulously.

"What?" Charles exclaimed, jerking his head toward her with his eyes wide open in amazement. "A woman?"

"I'm so shaken by this, I can't even begin to understand it," Sarah said. "Can you drive us home so you and I can go talk to Sophie? I really need to sit down and catch my breath."

"Well, that's the silliest thing I've heard this year," Sophie announced when they shared the news with her. "How could a woman do that much damage? They said Andy was severely battered. What woman could do that?" Then she hesitated and added, "… well, I guess I could." She appeared to be thinking about it for a minute, and then added, "But I didn't."

Ignoring Sophie's comment, Sarah said, "Well, Sophie, we have to admit that Andy was a slight person. There are women who could do him harm."

"Slight." Sophie bellowed. "If I hugged him, he would probably have broken." Sophie was putting two glasses on the coffee table and pouring wine for Sarah and Charles. She went back into the kitchen and returned with a platter of cheese and crackers and her own glass, already half empty.

"You just happened to have wine and cheese ready for us?" Sarah asked.

"No, I was having a solitary party, but I'm glad you two came. I'm not so glad you brought such troubling information … and that ugly dog."

"Why do you say 'troubling,' Sophie?" Charles asked, mostly just to see what she would say. He liked to practice his old skills occasionally.

"Because the only woman I know of in connection with Andy is Millie. And I don't even want to go there."

"Millie?" Sarah looked surprised that Sophie would consider Millie seriously even though they had offhandedly suggested her the previous day.

"And who would you suggest, Sarah?" Sophie asked.

"Hmm. Well … I don't know of anyone else really … but … Millie?" Sarah repeated skeptically. "Millie?"

"I think we need to talk to her again," Sophie announced.

"Now wait a minute," Charles interjected. "Wait just a minute. If you think she's the killer, then you should *not* be planning to talk to her. You should be talking to the detective assigned to this case."

"Spoken like a cop." Sophie bellowed. "No, we won't be talking to any detective. Besides, we've been told to stay out of it, so we can't talk to the police."

"Hold on," Charles said. "Staying out of the case means just that. It doesn't mean 'get involved, but don't tell the cops.' And that's for your own protection, you know," he added.

Sarah could tell Charles was getting agitated, and she signaled for Sophie to let it go. "Let's just relax tonight and let this information sink in. I don't think we should be making any decisions right now." Sophie gave her a slight nod, indicating that she understood. She knew they would pick the discussion up tomorrow morning, but without Charles.

"More wine, anyone?" Sophie asked innocently.

Chapter 40

Sophie and Sarah got up early the next day and took the local shuttle into town to get breakfast at the café. They offered a delicious country breakfast special there on Saturday mornings, and Sophie suggested that they both needed some comfort food. "I know your cute fellow doesn't approve of us getting involved in the investigation," Sophie was saying, "but I …"

At that moment, Millie walked in and rushed over to their table. "What's this all about, Sophie? Why was it so important for me to be here at exactly 9:30?"

Sarah looked at Sophie accusingly. She had clearly set up a meeting without telling Sarah, undoubtedly to avoid Charles's scrutiny. Sarah felt a bit guilty seeing Millie behind his back when she knew he was adamantly opposed to it. Sophie shrugged her shoulders, turning her palms up as if to say, "I did it. What can I say?"

Sarah responded by rolling her eyes. Then she turned to Millie and said, "Good morning, Millie. How are you today?"

"Confused," she responded. "What's going on?"

Sarah sat quietly looking at Sophie. This was clearly her meeting, and since they hadn't discussed it, she had no idea what Sophie had in mind. Sophie took another sip of her coffee and began. "Millie, we need to find out something from you, and we want you to be honest with us."

"Of course, Sophie. I've been honest with you so far."

"Not entirely, Millie. You didn't tell us you were at Andy's the night he was killed."

Sarah gasped but then coughed into her napkin, hoping to cover her surprise. They didn't know whether it had been Millie or not. Why was Sophie taking such a chance?

Millie dropped her eyes, and a tear ran down her left cheek. "No, Millie. No tears. Just talk to us," Sophie said coolly. Sarah felt bad for Millie. Sophie was taking a hard line with her. Millie wiped the tear away and sat quietly looking down at her hands. Sarah flagged the waitress and ordered a cup of tea for Millie. Millie glanced a 'thank you' toward Sarah.

After the tea arrived, Millie began to talk, but softly—almost too softly for Sarah to hear. She moved in closer. "Okay. I went to Andy's house earlier that evening. He was packing to go to his friend's place in Florida, and I was concerned about him. He had several phone calls that afternoon during our water aerobics class, and he seemed very upset. He left the class partway through and never came back. I tried to call him, but he didn't answer. I just wanted to make sure he was okay. He has seen me through so much turmoil over the years, and he never reached out when he had troubles himself," Millie explained. "I just wanted to hear from him that he was okay," she repeated.

"But why didn't you tell us that when we talked the other night?" Sophie asked.

"I'm sorry. I thought it would look bad. You both thought I was having an affair with him, and for me to say I was there would just confirm that in your minds. It was completely innocent."

"So, did you find out what was wrong?" Sophie asked.

"No. He said it was nothing important and that he was going to visit friends in Florida. He said the whole thing would blow over. He seemed to be in a hurry to get out of town, and I wondered about that, but he assured me everything was okay. That's why I called you that day after he was killed. I wanted someone to see if they could find out what he was so upset about. I tried to tell Detective Shields how upset Andy had been, but he didn't seem interested."

"Do the police know you were there?" Sarah asked, despite promising herself she would stay out of it.

"No. I was afraid to tell them that part because I knew what they would think. I was just hoping they would never find out. I guess I was afraid that if the police knew, Ralph would find out, and he would have been furious with me."

The women talked for a while when Millie suddenly stood up. "There's Ralph now. He dropped me off here and said he would be back for me in a half hour. I have to go." She looked nervous, excused herself, and left quickly. Ralph remained in the car but looked in at Sophie and Sarah. His eyes were cold.

As Sophie and Sarah were leaving the café, a police car rolled up. It had been sitting a half block away. Sarah had noticed it but didn't realize there was a driver inside. It pulled up beside them, and the window rolled down.

Officer Holmes was driving, and Detective Gabriel sat in the passenger seat. "Get in," the detective said.

"Excuse me," Sophie said with surprise. "Get in? Why?"

"We need to talk, and I would prefer we do it at the station."

He was wearing dark glasses and had not smiled. Amanda was looking straight ahead.

Sophie looked at Sarah questioningly, and Sarah answered in a whisper, "We should go." They got in the back seat. No one talked until they arrived at the police station and were seated in Detective Gabriel's office.

"Well," Detective Gabriel began, "I guess I'm finding out why Detective Shields was upset with you two."

Sophie sat tall and said defensively, "And why would that be, Detective Gabriel?"

"You are pursuing your own investigation and compromising ours." He said with thinly veiled anger. "There's a note in the Burgess file that Shields had considered arresting the two of you for interfering with a police investigation. I was astonished when I first saw that notation. Now I'm beginning to understand it."

"Could you please tell us what you think we've done wrong," Sophie asked with indignation.

"Well, for one thing, I just picked you up in front of the café where you were actively interviewing our witness, not to mention a person of interest to the department."

"A person of interest?" Sarah spoke up for the first time. "Are you looking at Millie for Andy's murder? But you arrested her husband, right?"

"Mrs. Miller. Everything you just asked me is police business. I will not be answering you. And you and your friend are forbidden to go near Mrs. Lake or her husband."

"*What?*" Sophie shouted. "We are 'forbidden'? Do you realize that Millie Lake is a friend of mine and has been for years? Who are you to *forbid* me. I absolutely refuse to stay away from my friend, and I would like to see what law you have that would permit you to tell me to do otherwise," Sophie stood up to leave.

"Okay, Mrs. Ward, calm down. I'll admit I misspoke when I said 'forbidden.' I shouldn't have said that, and I apologize." He still looked annoyed but seemed to be trying to restrain himself. "What I mean to say is this. Would you two women please just step down and let us do our job?" Sophie returned to her chair reluctantly.

"And are you doing that job?" Sophie asked, clearly still irritated.

"Trust me, Mrs. Ward. We're doing our job. That's how we happen to know you're interfering with it. I can't say any more than that and can only hope you'll honor my request."

"Humph." Sophie straightened her jacket and moved her purse to the opposite arm. She didn't look at the detective.

"I'm saying this for your own good, as well. You could be placing yourselves in danger." Sarah remembered Charles saying the same thing. Maybe they should listen.

Detective Gabriel asked Officer Holmes to drive the women back to the café, or to their homes if they preferred. Amanda led them to the squad car without speaking until they got in. She then turned to them and said, "Sorry about all that, ladies. He's a very nice man—nothing like Detective Shields. It's always hard when we're trying to solve several cases and keep innocent people safe at the same time. I hope you will listen to him."

"We will," Sarah said contritely.

Sophie poked Sarah and whispered, "Speak for yourself, kiddo. I have information about the scruffy man."

Chapter 41

When Sarah answered the phone, Charles began the conversation by asking, "Did you hear the news about your friend's husband?"

"Well, hello and a very good morning to you, too, my friend," Sarah responded. She then added curiously, "What news?"

"Okay. I'm sorry. I sometimes have a one-track mind when it comes to crimes and the justice system." Charles continued, "They had Lake's preliminary hearing yesterday, and the judge ruled there was insufficient evidence. They let him go."

"I guess that lawyer you recommended knew what he was doing," Sarah responded. "I knew he was innocent."

"Wait, Sarah. This doesn't mean he's innocent. It simply means the judge listened to the prosecution's case and didn't think the police had enough evidence to convict him. That's all it means. You continue to stay out of it, okay?"

"Sure, Charles. Of course," Sarah said innocently. "Would you like some breakfast?"

"I'll be right over," Charles responded enthusiastically.

"But I don't want to talk about the case, okay?" Sarah added, fearing he might ask about her involvement. She didn't want to admit to him what she and Sophie were up to.

An hour later the phone rang again. This time it was Sophie calling. "Is that lover boy's car I see over there?" she asked accusingly.

"Yes, Sophie. We're having breakfast."

"You aren't telling him about...."

"No, Sophie. Our plans are still on. I'll see you around five." Sarah cut the conversation short.

"What's that all about?" Charles asked when she got off the phone.

"Oh, that was just Sophie. We might do dinner ..." She hated lying to him. Actually, she wished he could go with them, but she knew he would object. It had to be done, so she quickly changed the subject. "Say. It's a beautiful day. Would you like to drive over by the river and take Barney for a walk? There's a nature walk along the bank that I think you would enjoy."

"Great idea." Charles said, "And Barney will love it. He's been a bit housebound lately. For that matter, so have I." Sarah was rinsing the dishes for the dishwasher. Charles came up from behind and wrapped his arms around her. She leaned back and settled into his embrace, which felt safe and caring. She slid around in his arms until she was facing him, and they melted into their first deep, loving kiss. Sarah rested her head on his chest, and they stood there quietly lost in the pleasure and in their own thoughts.

Later, as Sarah and Charles walked along the river path hand in hand, they didn't say much. There was a cool breeze, but the sun was warm and inviting. They took Barney's leash off when they came to a more isolated area and watched him leap around with excitement. He never got far from his family, always turning to make sure they were in sight. "He's really settled in, hasn't he?" Charles said. "You would never know he had been living on the street."

"I'm not sure he was on the street very long. He was so easy to train. I think he had a home at some point, or at least someone who loved him."

"How old is he?" Charles asked.

"No one really knows, but the vet thinks he might be around seven or eight." They had walked over a mile before they decided they should turn back. "Barney, come." He didn't come right away, so they headed toward where he was sniffing. Barney had wandered off the path and into the brush that divided the nature path from the old abandoned railroad tracks. Barney pushed through the grasses and disappeared into the overgrowth. "Barney, come here," Sarah demanded.

They followed him and immediately found themselves in a clearing, where they noticed several tarps tied to trees forming shelters. There was a rock fire pit and blankets and newspapers on the ground creating what Sarah thought might be sleeping areas. Barney was sniffing everywhere, and his tail was wagging wildly. "I wonder what Barney is so excited about," Sarah exclaimed. Turning to Charles, she asked, "Do you suppose people are actually living back here?"

"I wouldn't be surprised. There's no place in town for the homeless, and they have to sleep somewhere."

"I thought there was a shelter. Millie said Amanda told her about a shelter here in town."

"That's just for women and children," Charles responded. "There's nothing for men."

Sarah looked at him briefly with sorrow in her eyes. She then turned and called to Barney, "Come on, Barney. Let's go home." Barney left the area reluctantly. He was especially interested in an old flannel shirt tossed over a tree limb. Sarah snapped the leash on Barney, and the three made their way back to the path and started home. Sarah was very quiet.

"Are you okay?" Charles asked.

"Yes. I was just wondering what it must be like to live like that." They walked back to the car hand in hand. At the car, Sarah took two treats from her pocket and gave them to Barney. "You've been a good dog, Barney." He licked her hand and looked at her with love, but then he glanced longingly down the path they had just taken.

When they got home, Charles didn't go inside. He stopped by his car and pulled her to him for a gentle good-night kiss. They hadn't talked about the earlier kiss, but Sarah felt it would not be their last.

* * * * *

"I think we should take Barney with us," Sarah told Sophie. Then she added, "Are you sure we should be doing this?"

"Of course we should." It was dusk as they drove away from the house.

"I went there this morning," Sarah said casually.

"You *what*?" Sophie said, turning to Sarah abruptly. "What do you mean, 'you went there?'"

"Charles and I took a walk along the river, and Barney led us into the clearing."

"You didn't tell Charles what we're doing, did you?" Sophie asked accusingly.

"Of course not, Sophie. He would have stopped us. He would say we shouldn't be doing this ... and we both know we shouldn't ..."

"... and we both know we have to do it." Sophie finished Sarah's sentence.

"Yes, we do," Sarah said softly. Barney stretched his neck over the back of the seat and licked Sarah's cheek. "I love you, too, Barney. Lie down." She was glad she was bringing the dog.

"So, tell me about it," Sophie said as they drove to the river.

"Well," Sarah responded, "I'm just glad I've been there because I'm not sure we could find it in the dark. It's off the path back by the tracks. We might have spotted it if they have a fire going, but otherwise, I doubt it."

As they approached the parking area, Sarah said, "Let's drive on up the road and look for a closer place to park. We walked a long way before we came to it." Sarah knew Sophie wouldn't be able to walk that far. Sophie's knees and ankles were succumbing to arthritis, but she refused to use a cane or walker. They found a place to park, and there was even an access path with a sign pointing to the nature walk. Although it was still dusk, once they got to the path in the trees, it was dark. Sophie turned on her flashlight, and Barney led the way. He seemed to know exactly where they were going.

"When do you think the men come?"

"I would guess they get here before dark. You rarely see homeless people on the streets at night."

Barney started pulling at the leash and was very excited. Sarah kept him restrained, but he was eager to get loose. He headed straight for the clearing and practically dragged Sarah behind. "Slow down, Barney," she pleaded, but he continued on.

"Rusty," an old man yelled as they entered the clearing with Barney in the lead. He fell to the ground with his arms around the dog. "Welcome home, buddy. We've sure missed you." Barney licked his face wildly and wagged his whole body. "Where did you find him?" the man asked Sarah. Sarah stood in shock.

"You know this dog?" she asked.

"Sure. This is Rusty. He hangs out with us. He's been with us since he was a little bit of a thing. We found him behind the dumpster over by Barney's Bar & Grill." Turning to Barney, the man repeated, "Welcome home, buddy."

Sophie stood to the side not knowing what to say. Sarah, as well, was dumbfounded. This isn't what they came for.

"Where did you find him?" the man repeated.

"I got him at the pound," Sarah said. "He's been living with me for a while now."

"Well, he's sure been eating. Look at them ribs, Buck," he said turning to the other man in the clearing. "He's all filled out like he should be. You could count them ribs when he was with us," he added with a chuckle.

Sarah was sure the man was going to want him back, but she decided to put that aside for the time being and get on with the reason they came. "Do you know a Bob Pickett?" she asked. "By the way," she added. "I'm Sarah, and this is my friend, Sophie."

"Okay. What do you want with Bob?" the man asked, not introducing himself.

"We want to talk to him about a friend of his, Andy Burgess."

The man looked down and scratched the toe of his shoe around in the dirt. "What do you want to talk to him about Andy for?"

"We just want to talk. Andy was a good friend of ours, and we're trying to find out what happened to him." There was a small fire going in the fire pit. Two more men had entered the clearing from the railroad side. They made no noise and had obviously been waiting there. Sarah was beginning to realize this was a stupid thing for two women to do.

"What makes you think we know anything?" one of the men spoke up. Sarah looked at him as he moved out of the shadows. It was the scruffy man from the funeral. Sophie looked at her, and Sarah saw fear in her eyes. She didn't want the men to see it and was determined to remain strong herself. She didn't want them to sense her own fear.

"I don't know whether you do or not. We've just been talking to the people who knew Andy, the people who cared about him, hoping to find someone who knows what might have happened." She realized her hand was shaking, and she slipped it into her pocket. She was holding the leash with the other hand and gently guided Barney closer to herself. She realized, though, that if these men were to attack, she didn't know that Barney would help her since they were his friends as well. Actually, she didn't know if he would attack at all, he was such a gentle dog. The fire crackled. Everyone was quiet.

Finally the scruffy man spoke up. "I'm Bob," he said. "We all knew Andy." Everyone remained quiet. Sarah knew she needed to speak but didn't know what to say. Finally Sophie found her voice and spoke up.

"How did you know him?" she asked, not addressing anyone in particular. Again, there was quiet. Three of the men looked at Bob as if he were the person who should answer.

"I stop in at the AA meeting in town once in a while," Bob said, looking embarrassed. "Not that it helps much," he snorted.

"I wouldn't say it helps you much," one of the men said with a snicker. The other men laughed.

"Okay guys. Lay off," the scruffy man said with a frown. "Well, I met this Andy fellow there. He treated me like a regular guy, you know? He took me out for coffee after the meetings, and we talked just like normal people do. He made me feel good. We talked about our lives back when things were good. We told each other things we couldn't talk to other people about. I miss Andy. I went to his funeral, but I felt out of place and left right after the service." Sarah saw him there and felt sorry that she hadn't spoken to him. *How often do special people cross our paths and remain unnoticed?* she wondered.

Sarah saw a fallen tree nearby and knew Sophie's legs must be hurting. "Would it be okay for my friend and me to sit down?" she asked.

"Sure," one man said as he grabbed a blanket and spread it over a downed tree trunk for them. Sarah began to relax, realizing they were, most likely, in no danger. Sophie looked relieved to sit but said she would probably need help getting back up. The men assured her they would help. Sarah saw the fear had faded from Sophie's eyes.

The strange group sat around the fire and drank coffee out of tin cans. It was, by far, the worst coffee Sarah had ever tasted. She had boiled coffee grounds to make hobo coffee once many years ago just to see what it tasted like. This was even worse. But she was pleased they were talking. All the men had something to add about Andy. He had been to the clearing many times, bringing food and staying to eat with them. They all considered him a friend, but Bob seemed especially close to Andy.

The women stayed another hour sharing stories about Andy at first and learning about each other later. The men listened with interest as Sarah talked about losing her husband so suddenly. One of the men had lost his entire family in a tornado out west. He had traveled here to get away from the memories. "... but those dang things just follow you wherever you go," he had said, looking down as he spoke.

At some point, it became clear the men were spiking their coffee with whiskey, and they offered some to the women. Sarah thanked them but said she was driving. Sophie accepted with a smile but asked for just a little. Once she relaxed, Sophie told one of her raucous stories and had everyone howling with laughter. It was a good evening.

As they were preparing to leave, Sarah again wondered about Barney. He was off leash now and lying by the fire, looking right at home. As she stood, however, he stood, too. As she moved to leave the clearing, he was right at her heel. Sarah looked at the man who called him Rusty, and he just nodded his approval. She mouthed "thank you," and they headed out of the clearing and up the path by moonlight.

Chapter 42

"Your quilt is beautiful, Sarah. Let's hang it up in the shop." Sarah had wanted to take it home and see it on her couch, but if Ruth was willing to display it, that was quite an honor. "I want to show people what they can do with just a class or two. So many people come in and say they could never make a quilt, and just look what you did with hardly any experience." Ruth was very pleased with Sarah's work, and the machine quilter had done an exquisite job of quilting.

"Okay," Sarah said. "But let me take it now and bring it back in a couple of days. I really want to see it with my couch and show it to a couple of my friends."

"Of course. You take it home for as long as you want, Sarah. I know you must be very proud of this yourself. It's beautiful workmanship. How about I just borrow it from you the next time I run an advertisement for a class, okay?"

"Perfect," Sarah responded as she bundled it up to take home. She realized that her eyes were already scanning the bolts looking for that next quilt. "The next one I make will be for my bed," she said. Sarah headed for the pattern wall and thumbed through the books. She found one that particularly attracted her attention; however, it was not in colors she usually liked. For some reason, the quilt made her think of Charles.

"What can you tell me about this quilt?" she asked Ruth when the other customers had left.

"That's a civil war reproduction quilt. It's made from a pattern that was popular during the Civil War, and it's pieced using Civil War–reproduction fabrics."

"Do you carry the fabrics?" Sarah asked.

"Not those specific ones, but the fabrics in that section over there are all Civil War reproductions."

Sarah felt herself getting excited about the idea. A Civil War quilt would be a perfect gift for Charles. She had been thinking about making him a quilt at some point, but everything she looked at was so flowery and feminine. She hadn't even noticed the Civil War fabrics in the corner of the shop. "You might want to take this book," Ruth suggested. "It has your pattern and good instructions, but it also has a section on Civil War quilts that's interesting and well researched."

Sarah took the book but decided to wait to pick out the fabrics. She hadn't been inside Charles's house and didn't know what colors he might prefer. She went across the street to the café and sat down with a cup of tea and opened the book. She read that some of the quilts made during the Civil War period were extremely detailed with lots of appliqué and were designed to raise money for the war effort. But others were simple cot quilts and made quickly for their men to take with them. Tears came to her eyes as she read that many of these men and boys were wrapped in their blood-stained quilts when they were buried.

She decided to follow one of the cot patterns but to make it wider. Most authentic cot quilts were long and narrow to fit the soldiers' cots, but she wanted Charles to be able to use it on his bed. She wondered about his bed but quickly stopped wondering because that caused her mind to wander into areas she was still avoiding. Instead, she started reading about the pattern she liked and discovered that, in addition to the cot size, there were instructions for other sizes, including a full-queen. She decided that would probably be just right.

"You're back," Ruth said with surprise as Sarah returned to the shop. "Did you forget something?"

Sarah smiled and said, "Remember that fabric I was going to buy later? Well, I guess it's 'later' because I'm back to get it." Both women laughed. Sarah spent almost two hours pulling bolts out and lining them up on the cutting table. She decided it didn't matter about his colors because this was going to be a scrap quilt made of many colors. The blocks were made of four patches set on point with setting triangles. They were arranged in lengthwise strips separated by a wide sashing strip. She wasn't sure about the setting triangles, but Ruth assured her it would be easy once she learned how.

Sarah chose a tone-on-tone green for the sashing strips and a brown for the setting triangles. The four patches were made from the many fat quarters she chose to give it a scrappy look. "It's hard to believe woman were able to throw this quilt together overnight."

"Don't forget, in those days, quilts were made by all the women in the family, plus their friends and neighbors. Also, don't forget that you have the Friday night group to help out."

Sarah left excited about her project. She didn't realize it was nighttime already. She was glad she brought her car, not only because it was dark, but because she now had a large bag of fabric to carry.

Sarah arrived home later than usual and had neglected to leave the outside light on. She had trouble lining the key up with the lock but then realized the door was slightly ajar. "It wasn't even closed? How can that be?" she said aloud.

She heard Barney barking as he rushed to the door. He nervously ran back and forth between Sarah and her bedroom door. "What is it, Barney? Are you pretending to be Lassie?" she teased. "Is Timmy in the well?"

Barney didn't smile. He was tense and continued to pace between Sarah and the door to her bedroom.

Thinking about the front door being ajar, she suddenly became tense herself. *Is someone in the house?*

She turned the lights on in the living room and picked up her umbrella. Then she put it down, realizing that it was too flimsy to be of any protection. She picked up the ceramic umbrella stand instead and approached the bedroom door.

She saw the outline of a man as she reached for the light switch and clicked it on. Her dresser drawers had been emptied onto the floor, and the man had pulled everything out of the closet. Her suitcases were open and scattered around the room. The mattress had been pulled off the bed.

The man turned, and she saw his face. Her legs went weak, and the ceramic jar crashed to the floor as she started to fall. She grabbed for the door frame to steady herself.

The man lunged for her, she screamed, and Barney lunged for the man.

One second later the man was on his back, and Barney had him by the throat. A low growl emerged from deep within Barney's throat. The man didn't move, and neither did Barney. Sarah watched with disbelief.

"Andy?" she asked cautiously. "Is that you?"

"Yes, it's me," he said struggling to get free. "Get this dog off me before he kills me."

"But Andy … you're dead. I was at your funeral." She tried to get her thoughts together but couldn't make sense of what she was seeing. Andy appeared to be on her floor beneath Barney, but she knew it couldn't be possible. "I saw Andy in his casket. I saw him lowered into the ground," she cried. "You're not Andy. Who are you?" *Am I losing my mind? Is this a hallucination?*

"Sarah, I implore you. Get this creature off of me. I can feel his teeth closing on my throat. He's going to kill me."

"Tell me first who you are," Sarah demanded with a trembling voice.

The man hesitated, for he knew the dog was capable of killing him in an instant. He had to get Sarah calm enough to call the dog off. He lay very still and tried to relax his muscles, knowing the dog would sense the change. As he did, he felt the dog relax ever so slightly.

"I'm Andy, and I'm not dead. It was a mistake." He said gently. After a few moments, he continued, "I came for the quilt, Sarah. That's all. I came to get the quilt and leave before anyone saw me. Please Sarah, the dog? I'll explain when I get up."

Sarah listened. *A mistake?* She knew there was no mistake. He was dead, buried, and mourned. She was there. But she needed to hear what this man had to say. And she didn't know for sure that Barney wouldn't kill him. She decided to call the dog off, knowing he would come to her rescue if the man made a wrong move. "Barney, it's okay. Come here."

Barney reluctantly removed his mouth from the man's throat and moved to the side, but he didn't go to Sarah. He stayed within inches of the man's face. The man began to move very slowly. Barney crouched low and growled. His lips quivered, and his teeth glistened.

"It's okay, Barney," Sarah said. "Let the man up." The man slowly rose to his knees but stopped when he heard the growl intensify. He watched the dog cautiously. The dog stood with his front legs apart, slightly bent forward. His lips quivered. Saliva slithered from between his teeth and fell to the floor.

The man looked at Sarah pleadingly and said, "Please Sarah. Where's my quilt? That's all I came for, and I'll leave."

"Tell me who you really are," Sarah demanded while trembling and still holding onto the wall for balance. Then it hit her. "Wait. I know. You're his brother." She had heard he had a brother, and she thought she remembered that he was a twin. *That could explain it*, she thought.

"Of course," Sarah exclaimed with growing confidence. "That's who you are. You're Andy's brother." She felt relieved for a moment once she knew she wasn't dealing with the living dead but then remembered that his brother was in prison for murder. If this was his brother, then she was alone with a murderer. She tensed up again, and Barney followed suit.

"Stay away from me," she demanded, looking toward Barney for support. Barney, again, began to growl.

"I'm Andy, Sarah. I don't know how I can prove it. Wait, yes I do. Sophie introduced us...." He paused and then added eagerly, "... I taught you how to use the computer ... we went to the community pool together ..." He paused again to see her reaction. She was listening. "See, Sarah. I know you." The man slowly got up on his feet watching Barney as he moved. Barney continued to growl and never took his eyes off the man. "I'm Andy," the man said again, softly. "Please believe me, Sarah."

"Then explain how I saw you in the coffin. I just don't understand. Are you alive? Are you real?" She felt herself becoming hysterical again and knew she had to maintain control. "I have to call Sophie," she said, moving toward the living room.

"Stop Sarah," the man demanded. She froze, and Barney tensed. Then in a softer tone, he said, "I know I've frightened you, Sarah. And I'm so very sorry. Please, let's go into the living room and sit down. I'll explain everything, you can get the quilt for me, and I promise to leave as long as you promise not to tell anyone I was here." He then muttered to himself, "It just might work as long as no one else sees me."

"And if I just start screaming?"

"I guess I would have to kill you," he responded reluctantly. Sarah noticed he was beginning to tremble.

"You would kill me? You would actually kill me?" Sarah said in disbelief. "Then you are certainly not Andy. Andy would never kill me. He's no killer. That means you *must* be his brother. He's the killer." She was inching her way toward the living room, and the man was doing the same while keeping a close eye on the dog.

Barney moved with them but remained close to the man. When the man reached the living room, Barney posted himself two feet away, and the low growl continued to exude from deep within his throat.

Suddenly, the man began to look disoriented. Sweat ran down his forehead, and his hands shook. "Oh god, what am I doing?" Sarah lowered herself onto the couch slowly. The man collapsed next to her with his face in his hands. Barney moved closer to him, and his raised lip began to quiver.

Turning to Sarah, the man pleaded, "Sarah, please believe me. I'm Andy. You didn't see me dead. That was my brother, George. I killed him." He began to sob.

"Your brother George?" she asked skeptically. "But the body was found in your house. We all thought ..."

"I know. I know." His hands covered his face as he shook his head side to side in resignation and continued to sob. "I know." Tears streamed down his cheeks. "I knew you all thought I was dead, and I let you think that." He attempted to pull himself together as he wiped at the tears with his shirt sleeve. He looked at her apologetically. "I've hurt everyone I care about."

He paused and then added pleadingly, "I'm in such a mess, Sarah. I've done everything wrong. You were my friend, and I'm so sorry I hurt you, and I'm sorry I frightened you tonight. I don't want to hurt anyone anymore. But please let me explain."

Sarah's head was beginning to clear. She looked into his eyes and realized this was definitely Andy sitting next to her. She knew him, and she could sense his compassion. George may be a killer, but this man was not. The man sitting next to her was suffering from guilt and fear. She knew this was Andy. But what, she wondered …

She put her hand on his shoulder and softly said, "Andy." He turned to her, and she put her arm around him.

He laid his head against her chest and sobbed, "What have I done? What have I done?"

Sarah sat with him and let him sob until he became still. He finally lifted his head and said he was sorry. "I hate being like this, Sarah. I'm so sorry. I've been so confused, and I don't know how to straighten things out. I don't even think it's possible."

"Would you feel better if you had the quilt in your hands?" Sarah asked.

"I guess. I kept thinking the quilt could help me solve my problems, but I know that's not true anymore." Andy hung his head and looked utterly defeated.

"I think you should go get the quilt. I'll hold Barney here so he doesn't attack you again. Okay?" Sarah suggested, while gently guiding Barney close to her legs holding his collar. She pushed Andy's hair off his forehead and gently patted his cheek. "Go get it and we'll talk more."

"Okay," Andy said reluctantly. "Where is it?"

"Go into my sewing room. It's to the left of the bathroom," she said, pointing toward the room. "In that room, you'll see a large oak cabinet. Your quilt is on the bottom shelf under a couple of blankets."

"Will you wait right here?" he asked with fear in his voice. His hands were trembling.

"Of course I will. I'll be right here holding Barney," she assured him.

Andy walked toward the sewing room but looked back to be sure Barney wasn't following him. A few moments later Sarah heard him open the cabinet doors. Sarah carefully slipped the cell phone from her pocket and pressed "1." When Charles answered, she whispered, "Come quickly. Don't knock. Just come in silently. I need your help." She pressed the off button and quickly returned the phone to her pocket. She felt a pang of disloyalty because Andy trusted her, but she wasn't sure she could trust him.

Sarah, still holding Barney's collar, moved into the kitchen and took a platter of roast beef out of the refrigerator. She got bread from the bread box and began making two sandwiches. She poured a large glass of milk.

"Where did you go?" Andy shouted apprehensively as he returned to the living room. Barney tensed and, again, began to growl. Sarah held his collar and reassured him.

"I'm in the kitchen, Andy. It's okay. Come in here, and we'll have a bite to eat and talk. I made you a sandwich and a glass of milk." He stared at the table as if he didn't know what to do next. "Sit down, and we'll talk. I want to know everything that happened. We'll figure this out together like you said." Sarah, seeing that he was still trembling, tried to appease him, knowing that he was on the edge and could lose control at any moment.

He sat but didn't move toward the food. "Can I get you something different?" Sarah asked.

"I just want to get myself together. I can't think. Could we, maybe, have some coffee?" he asked timidly.

"Of course," she said gently to the man who had just threatened her life. *Am I crazy to trust him?*

She started the coffee and placed two cups on the table. She wondered if he might have a gun. The image of Charles walking in and Andy shooting him flashed across her mind, and for a moment she wished she hadn't called. But then she realized that he probably didn't have a gun, or he would have pulled it out by now. She hoped she hadn't placed Charles's life in danger. And she hoped she wasn't placing her own life in danger.

"Do you want to open the quilt box?" Sarah asked.

"No. I want to explain what I've done. The quilt doesn't even matter anymore." Andy hung his head and looked dejected.

"Talk when you feel like it, Andy," she said softly as she joined him at the table.

"I don't know where to start." Barney sat vigilantly about two feet from Andy's chair. He never took his eyes off Andy.

"Start at the beginning," Sarah said. "The last time I saw you, you were going away for a few days, and you left your quilt with me. Start there."

"Yes, the quilt." He started to become agitated again. "Maybe I should take it and go."

"Andy, please just talk. You said you would tell me what happened. You have the quilt. It's yours. But it would be cruel to leave me without explaining what happened to you and whose funeral I went to."

"Okay. Well, I left the quilt here and went home to pack for my trip to Florida." He became quiet. He sipped his coffee, but the food remained untouched. After a few minutes, he continued. "No … it started before that. My brother called that afternoon. I thought he was still in prison, but he said he had been released. He probably escaped, but whatever. Anyway, he said he wanted the tie quilt. I asked him why, and he said it was none of my business. We argued. It wasn't really a big thing. He could have the quilt. It was just the way he was demanding it. It made me mad, and I told him he couldn't have it. We never got along." He fooled with his shirt sleeve and his watch. He was becoming agitated again.

Sarah listened intently, both to Andy and for signs of Charles coming in. "Go on …"

"So anyway, I had already gone to bed. It was sometime around 1:00 in the morning that I heard him banging on the door. He was drunk and loud. I opened the door, and he pushed past me and starting tearing up my house. He kept demanding to have the quilt. By the way, Sarah," he said, looking up at Sarah with sorrow in his eyes. "I'm so very sorry I involved you in this, but that's the reason I brought the quilt to your house. I was afraid he would come after it."

"Why did he want the quilt so badly?" she asked.

"Well, he finally told me, but he was yelling and tearing up my place while he talked. He said our grandfather had left a lot of money, but he didn't trust banks. He put it in a safe deposit box somewhere. He said grandma sewed the key into the tie quilt. I don't know how he knew that. I never heard that story. It might not even be true."

"What does this have to do with your not being dead?" Sarah asked. As she spoke, she heard a sound in the living room. She said, "Oh, the coffee is ready," and she hopped up to fill the cups as a distraction so Andy didn't notice the sound. But she had forgotten about Barney, who went running into the living room wagging his tail and greeting Charles enthusiastically. Andy jumped up and grabbed a carving knife from the knife block on the counter. When Charles turned the corner he was facing Andy and the knife.

Sarah's heart sank. She could only hope that his experience as a police officer would help him to defuse the situation. Andy was again panicking. "Who are you?" Andy demanded. His hand trembled so bad that the knife was in constant motion.

"He's a friend of mine, Andy," Sarah said calmly. "A good friend. He can help us figure this out. Please, just let him sit down at the table with us. He's a very smart man. He can help."

"Andy?" Charles said skeptically, looking at Sarah. "Not the *dead* Andy?"

"Yes, Charles. As it turns out, Andy isn't actually dead."

"This should be good." Turning to Andy, he said, "That shaking knife makes me really nervous. Do you think you could at least lay it down on the table over there? Right now it's pointing at me, and I have a nervous stomach. You know how that is …" he said congenially.

As Andy glanced toward the table nervously, Charles used his cane to hit the arm holding the knife. Barney jumped right into the ruckus and, again, had Andy on the floor by his throat.

Charles looked down at the two. He looked at Sarah and calmly asked, "Do you think Barney will kill him?"

"I don't know, Charles. He didn't the last time," she said smiling. They let Andy cool his heels for a while, lying very still under Barney. Finally, Sarah said, "Charles. This is Andy Burgess. He's not dead. His brother is dead—his twin brother. That's why we thought it was Andy."

"He was just telling me what happened when you came in. I hope you won't hold it against him that he pulled a knife on you. He threatened my life, too, but he apologized." She was clearly making light of the situation, trying to defuse the tension. "Let's let him get on with his story." Charles reluctantly agreed but didn't find the situation at all amusing.

"It's okay, Barney. Let him up," Sarah said. Barney slowly moved off of Andy but growled whenever Andy made a move. "Come over here, Barney." He reluctantly moved to her side, still watching Andy's every move.

"You can get up, Andy, but do it slowly," Sarah said. "Sit back down, and I would appreciate it if you would apologize to my friend. He can be a big help to us in figuring out what to do next."

"Sorry, man. I don't know what's wrong with me." Andy hung his head. Charles was not moved by the apology but gave a short nod.

While Andy sat with his head hanging, Sarah caught Charles up on everything that had happened so far. She saw anger in his eyes when she talked about coming in to find him in the house. She touched his leg gently with her foot to get his attention and shook her head almost imperceptibly. He understood.

"Okay, Andy, please go on," Sarah said gently. "Your brother was ransacking your house and yelling about the quilt. He told you he wanted it because of a key that might be in it that may or may not lead to your grandfather's fortune."

"Well … maybe not a fortune," Andy admitted. "I actually don't know how much is involved, but for George to get so crazy I figured it was a sizable amount."

"So what happened to your brother?" Charles asked, trying to sound patient. "What was his name again?"

"George. George Burgess," Andy said. "He was no good. We never got along and fought all the time as kids. He fought with everybody—ended up in jail three or four times 'til he finally got life for killing a guy in a bar. I guess he got out somehow. Anyway, we started fighting, and we were both seeing red. We slammed each other all over the room. In the end, he fell and didn't get up. I looked, and there was blood everywhere. His head hit on something—the edge of the fireplace, I guess."

"Was he dead?" Charles asked.

"Yeah, man. He was totally dead." Andy lowered his head, and tears began to run down his cheeks. He spoke softly, "He was my brother, and no matter how bad a guy he was, he was still my brother, and I killed him."

Everyone was quiet for a while. Andy reached for a napkin and wiped his face. With his head lowered, he glanced up at Charles, looking embarrassed.

"What did you do next?" Charles asked.

"I got in his car," Andy said, "and shot out of here like a madman."

"The white car," Sarah said softly. "That was Andy leaving." Then she remembered the white car on the tape coming into the Village. "… and that wasn't Andy testing someone's car," she added enthusiastically. "That was Andy's brother pretending to be Andy so he could drive into the Village."

Charles, determined not to be sidetracked by Sarah's epiphany about the white car, said to Andy, "And then?"

"And then I did the stupidest thing there was to do," Andy continued. "I continued to run because I was scared. I drove south until I got to my friends' house in Orlando."

"Then my sister called." He continued. "I nearly had a stroke when they answered the phone, and it was her. I thought she had found me, but it turned out she was calling to tell my friends I was dead. I grabbed the phone and hung up before they had a chance to tell her any different."

"That's when I found out that you folks thought that was me lying there. It was a strange feeling. I wasn't wanted for murder—I was *dead*."

"What about the fingerprints?" Charles asked, but of course no one in the room knew the answer to that question. "What did you do next?" Charles asked, deciding to put the question of the fingerprints aside.

"I stayed with them for a couple of months. We drank and played cards. I tried to put it all out of my mind."

"But then one day I told them what happened—the whole story. We talked about it, and it seemed like the right thing to do was to come up here and get the quilt, get the money, and leave the country. Partly it was the alcohol scrambling my brain. I'm not used to drinkin' anymore. Anyway, I sobered up and headed back here."

"But now that I'm here …" He continued contritely, "It just doesn't seem like the right thing to do anymore. I should have stayed in the first place and faced the music." Andy raised his head and looked directly at Charles. "Maybe that's what I should do now."

Charles was quiet for a while. Then he said, choosing his words carefully, "Well, Andy. It was an accident. And as an accident, you probably would have gotten off at the time. But now I don't know. You left the scene. I don't know …"

Charles seemed to be drawing out his words, killing time. Sarah wondered what he was doing. Charles continued speaking slowly, "You're right that you need to face up to what you did, but it doesn't sound to me like you killed him purposely. But you did run." He looked upward, appearing to be thinking, then added, "You could be charged with involuntary manslaughter, I suppose. But since you ran, well that could raise it to a felony I guess." Charles continued to speak slowly and deliberately. "You would get some time in that case. A good lawyer might get you off. But if it were me, I would rather take my chances with the law than spend the rest of my life as a fugitive …"

"I wouldn't be a fugitive, would I?" Andy interjected. "Everyone thinks I'm dead."

"But you aren't dead, are you?" The voice came from the doorway as a tall, impeccably dressed man with finely chiseled features stepped into the kitchen, followed by two uniformed officers.

"Detective Gabriel," he said, introducing himself. "And you must be the infamous Andrew Burgess. I'm pleased to find you alive," he said with a smile. Then turning to one of the police officers behind him, he said, "Cuff him and read him his rights."

Charles turned to Sarah and, with a sparkle in his eye, whispered, "I get chills every time I hear those words."

Sarah didn't find it amusing and was upset with everyone. She gave Charles an irritated look for calling Gabriel, but immediately her face softened because she knew he had done the right thing.

She told Andy she was sorry it ended this way and assured him that she and Charles would do everything they could to help him.

Andy said he was glad to get it over with. Sarah could tell that he meant it.

For the first time that night, she could see the *old Andy* in his eyes. She gave him a hug and whispered in his ear, "I'll keep the quilt for you."

He smiled and winked.

As the officers led Andy from the room, the telephone rang.

"What the Sam Hill is going on over there?" Sophie yelled. "What are all those cop cars doing out front?"

"Get over here, Sophie. Do I ever have a story for you."

TIE DIED

See full quilt on back cover.

Sarah Miller plans to make a remembrance quilt from her husband's ties for their daughter, Martha. Make this 45½″ × 45½″ quilt for someone special in your life.

MATERIALS

Silk ties: 20–25 in assorted colors

Accent fabric: 1¼ yards (¾ yard for sashing, ½ yard for binding)

Foundation paper, such as Carol Doak's Foundation Paper (by C&T Publishing): 32 pieces

Backing: 3 yards

Batting: 53″ × 53″

Project Instructions

Seam allowances are ¼″. WOF = width of fabric.

MAKE THE BLOCKS

> **Tip** ‖ A damp pressing cloth between the silk ties and your iron will prevent damage to the silk and help remove set-in wrinkles.

1. Use masking tape to join 2 sheets of foundation paper. Trim to 10½″ × 10½″. Make 16.

> **Tip** ‖ A short stitch length throughout (15–20 per inch) will keep your stitches secure when removing the foundation paper.

2. Remove the stitching from the back of the ties. Open them and iron flat.

3. Place a tie, right side up, across the diagonal center of a foundation-paper square.

4. Pin another tie, right side down, on top of the first tie, matching the long edges.

5. Sew along the matched long edge through the ties and the paper. Press. Trim along the edges of the foundation paper.

6. Repeat Steps 4 and 5 until the foundation paper is completely covered. Trim block to 10″ × 10″. Make 16 blocks.

MAKE THE SASHING

1. Cut 11 strips of sashing, each 2″ × WOF.

2. Sew 6 strips together at the narrow ends. Press. Trim 5 long sashing strips, each 2″ × 46″.

3. From the remaining 5 strips, cut 20 short sashing strips, each 2″ × 10″.

ASSEMBLE AND FINISH THE QUILT

1. Sew 4 blocks and 5 short sashing strips into each row. Press.

2. Sew together 4 rows and 5 long sashing strips. Press.

3. Remove the foundation paper from the back of the blocks.

4. Layer the pieced top with the batting and backing. Quilt and bind as desired.

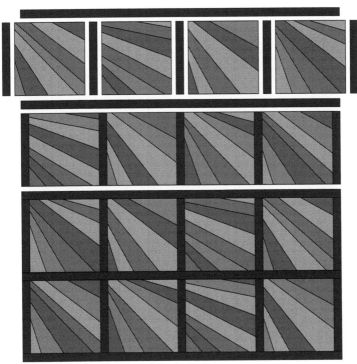

Quilt assembly

Turn the page for a preview ----------------------------▶
of the next book in A Quilting Cozy series.

2nd edition includes instructions to make the featured quilt

Running Stitches

a quilting cozy

Carol Dean Jones

Preview of
Running Stitches

There was no trial. Andy agreed to a plea bargain and was sentenced to five years in the local minimum-security prison farm. It was clear to everyone that Andy was no criminal. He killed his brother in the equivalent of a bar fight, which took place in Andy's living room. George had burst in, belligerent and angry, and they'd fought as they had since they were young boys.

It was an accident, and Andy probably wouldn't have been charged if he hadn't left town. But he returned home and was arrested. Andy was sorry about killing his brother, but he was mostly sorry that they'd never resolved their differences. He missed his brother, or maybe he just missed the idea of a brother. Andy was a kind and caring man.

No one expected that Andy would escape, but that's exactly what he did.

* * * * *

"It's spectacular!" Sarah exclaimed as Ruth and her daughter Katie hung the quilt behind the cash register.

"I've never seen a quilt like that! What's it called?" Sarah was a new quilter and had limited exposure to the world of quilts.

"This is called a sampler. We used fabrics from the Civil War–reproduction collection and these are all blocks that were popular during the mid-1800s," Ruth explained.

Katie spoke up saying, "It's possible that some of these blocks were used by the Underground Railroad as secret codes to communicate with runaway slaves."

"Fascinating!" Sarah said. "I'd love to know more about that."

"We'll be talking about all this in our next class," Ruth responded. "In fact," she added as she stood back and admired the quilt, "this would be a good quilt for you to make, Sarah, since you would learn all these different techniques."

"I love it," Sarah exclaimed.

Ruth Weaver owned Running Stitches, or as her customers fondly called it, Stitches. Ruth and Katie, her twenty-year-old daughter, provided a wide range of high-end quilting fabrics, all the necessary tools and implements, and an endless supply of books and patterns. The walls of the shop were covered with quilts made primarily by Katie who, along with her mother, taught classes for both the advanced quilter and those with nothing more than a desire to learn.

Sarah had been in that last category. After her husband died, she had saved his ties, hoping to use them to make a quilt for her daughter, Martha. Unfortunately, Sarah had no idea where to start and came to Stitches as a novice. Ruth and Katie had patiently guided her through the fundamentals and, as a result, Sarah had become quite proficient.

"Wouldn't this be too advanced for me?" Sarah asked.

"No. I'm calling this an advanced class, but I'll be teaching the simplest blocks first and, by the time we get to the more difficult blocks, you'll be ready."

Sarah examined the quilt more closely. "I bought many of these fabrics for the quilt I was planning for Charles."

"Have you used those fabrics yet?" Ruth asked.

"No," Sarah responded, thinking about the quilt she was planning to make for her friend, Charles. "Maybe I'll sign up for this class and make this one for him instead. It's historical, and I think he would like that."

Sarah and Charles had met many years before she moved to Cunningham Village; he was the policeman who came to her door almost twenty years ago to inform her of the accident that had taken the life of her husband, Jonathan. Despite the anguish of that day, the kindness of this gentle man stood out. After she moved to the Village, they met again. He was retired, as was she, and both were starting a new chapter of their lives.

"He's smitten," her feisty friend, Sophie, had said the day she met him. Sarah was not at all ready for *smitten* and tried hard not to give Charles any encouragement. But she liked him and he'd become a very special friend.

Sarah had moved to Cunningham Village the previous year at the insistence of her daughter, Martha, and against her own better judgment. But as it turned out, Martha was absolutely right.

Cunningham Village was a retirement community with independent villas, a center with all the recreational and educational services a person could want, and a continuing care component, which was available to seniors who needed more care.

That was Sarah's original objection—the concept of a retirement village made her feel old. Or maybe, in her late sixties, it was just a reminder that *old* was a state rapidly approaching. But once she made the move, got to know her neighbors, and got involved in the activities, she quickly adjusted to her new life. Quilting had become an essential part of that new life.

After signing up for the class and buying a few more fabrics from Ruth's Civil War collection, Sarah drove home, again turning her thoughts to Charles. They were clearly becoming close, but she wasn't sure just where she wanted it to go. But, wherever it was headed, she knew she wanted it to go there slowly.

Jonathan had been her first and only love and, for some reason she couldn't explain, her growing relationship with Charles was causing her to feel disloyal to Jon's memory. She felt that Charles would understand. He had lost his wife many years ago and still looked wistful when he talked about her.

All of Sarah's concerns vanished when she opened her front door and was met by the enthusiasm and love of her precious dog, Barney. Barney ran in circles and snuggled in close to her with every muscle trembling in an attempt to keep from jumping up on her. "Good boy, Barney!" She told him, appreciating his effort. "Let's go for a walk." Barney ran to the hook and tugged on his leash, dragging it to her and dropping it at her feet. "Good boy," she repeated, clapping her hands. Barney smiled.

Sarah adopted Barney from the local Humane Society the previous year. There had been a murder on her block, and she originally wanted him for protection, but they'd become fast friends. He was a medium-size dog of no particular, recognizable breed. He had big brown eyes, almost the color of his coat. He was ever so slightly cross-eyed. He had a long snout of a nose and rather longish whiskers that twitched when he opened his mouth. When Sarah first saw him, she thought he was undoubtedly the homeliest dog she had ever seen, but he was most certainly smiling at her. Sarah had looked at his short wagging tail, his straggly coat, and she smiled back. He looked at her with appreciation. They'd made an instant connection. She had to have him. He had to have her.

Together they went out into the brisk night air and strolled up the block. The homes on her block, as well as on most of the blocks in the Village, were one-story villas attached in groups of five. As she passed Andy's empty house, she thought about the tragedy that occurred there the previous year, resulting in Andy being sentenced to a few years in prison. She was eager for the day he'd be back home. She missed her friend.

"What're you and that ugly dog doing out there in the middle of the night?" Sophie hollered from her door. She already had her pink elephant pajamas on and had her trench coat over her shoulders as she walked toward them.

"I could ask the same question of you. You look like you're ready for bed," Sarah responded, "… and Barney's not ugly!" she added.

Sophie walked hurriedly toward Sarah and Barney. Sophie was a short rotund woman in her mid-seventies. She had an infectious laugh that could be heard up and down the block as she told her greatly embellished versions of the many happenings around the Village.

Sophie was also one of the kindest people Sarah had ever met. She took newcomers under her wing and helped them with what could be a particularly traumatic experience as they moved into a retirement community. She had been Sarah's first friend and they'd remained close. Right now, however, Sophie looked worried.

"I need to tell you something, and it's not good news, Sarah."

Sarah stopped walking and turned to meet Sophie. Barney stretched out on the sidewalk and rested his head on his front paws. "What is it, Sophie?" Sarah asked with apprehension.

"That young policewoman called me today and asked if we've had any contact with Andy."

"We talk to him every few weeks! Did you tell her that?" Sarah asked frowning. "Why does she want to know anyway?"

"I told her about our phone calls to the prison. That wasn't what she wanted to know. She wanted to know if he has been around here."

"Around here?" Sarah responded looking bewildered. "How could he have been around here? He's in prison."

"That's just it," Sophie said as she glanced down to hide the tears that were beginning to collect in her eyes. "He escaped, Sarah."

"*What?*" Sarah cried out. "How could he do that?" Andy was scheduled to be released in a couple of years and, with good behavior, maybe sooner. "He's ruined it for himself again! What's wrong with that man?" Sarah was clearly upset and disappointed with Andy. She and Sophie had stood by him through his trial and tried to make prison life easier for him by writing and phoning often. "He hasn't said a word that would suggest this was on his mind," she added with a deep frown. "Why would he do it?"

"How well do we really know Andy?" Sophie asked rhetorically. "He's been a great friend and neighbor, but there's much about Andy we don't know." It was during the investigation that Sophie and Sarah had first learned about Andy's history with alcohol. Then he ran off to Florida rather than admit to the fight he had with his brother that resulted in his brother's death. "And don't forget," Sophie added, "he let us think he was dead for several months! That was not kind!" Sophie was obviously disappointed with Andy.

Sarah shook her head and sighed. "Let's get some sleep, Sophie. We'll talk tomorrow, and we'll call that policewoman. What was her name, Amanda? Amanda something?"

"Amanda Holmes. She's still working with Detective Gabriel. Maybe we can go by and talk to both of them. This is just crazy!" Sophie said, shaking her head as she turned to leave. "Why would he do this?" she muttered to herself.

Sophie headed toward her house without saying goodbye. Sarah was confused by the news. At first, she felt angry with Andy but then realized there must be some explanation. She hoped she would find out soon. The previous year, she'd spent many weeks worrying about what had happened to Andy. She and Sophie even got involved in the investigation, much to the police department's annoyance. She wasn't eager to start worrying about him again. Sarah slowly headed for her front door. Barney got up, stretched, and lumbered after her.

Sarah turned and watched the house across the street as Sophie's lights went off, one after the other as she made her way toward her bedroom. Sarah sighed and said, "Come on, Barney. Let's get some sleep. I think tomorrow is going to be a long day." Barney sighed and followed her into the house.

A Note
from the Author

I hope you enjoyed *Tie Died* as much as I enjoyed writing it. This is the first book in A Quilting Cozy series and is followed by *Running Stitches*, which picks up with our characters just a few months later.

On page 234, I have included a preview to *Running Stitches* so that you can get an idea of what our cast of characters will be involved in next.

In the meantime, I'd love to hear from you. Please contact me on my blog or send me an email to the address below.

Best wishes,

Carol Dean Jones
caroldeanjones.com
quiltingcozy@gmail.com

READER'S GUIDE:
A QUILTING COZY SERIES
by Carol Dean Jones

1. How do you feel about Sarah's family insisting that she give up her home and move to a retirement community?

2. Sarah got into quilting by wanting to preserve her husband's ties, but quilting ended up playing a large part in her adjustment to her new life. What other actions helped her make a successful transition to life in a retirement community? What about her personality helped her make these changes?

3. How did Detective Shields' alcoholism affect his profession and his personal life? Do you think anyone could have helped him face his addiction?

4. How did adopting Barney affect Sarah's life?

5. Why do you think Millie refused to press charges against her abusive husband? Why do you think some people choose to remain with their abusers?

6. How has reading this book affected your opinion of living in a retirement community?